PURRFECT VIRUS

THE MYSTERIES OF MAX 79

NIC SAINT

PURRFECT VIRUS

The Mysteries of Max 79

Copyright © 2023 by Nic Saint

All rights reserved. No part of this book may be reproduced in any form by any electronic or mechanical means including photocopying, recording, or information storage and retrieval without permission in writing from the author.

This is a work of fiction. Names, characters, places, brands, media, and incidents are either the product of the author's imagination or are used fictitiously. The author acknowledges the trademarked status and trademark owners of various products referenced in this work of fiction, which have been used without permission. The publication/use of these trademarks is not authorized, associated with, or sponsored by the trademark owners.

Edited by Chereese Graves

www.nicsaint.com

Give feedback on the book at: info@nicsaint.com

facebook.com/nicsaintauthor
@nicsaintauthor

First Edition

Printed in the U.S.A

PURRFECT VIRUS

Going Viral

When our humans started getting sick and before long fell into a deep coma, we frankly feared for our lives, especially when the disease took out half of Hampton Cove's population and for a moment it looked as if the four of us were the last ones standing. As it was, the members of the neighborhood watch had been spared, and so Gran, Scarlett, Wilbur and Father Reilly took it upon themselves to find out what was going on. Especially when it transpired that the virus was man-made and certain dark forces had launched it with a specific and nefarious goal in mind.

And so four senior citizens and their seven cats began a campaign to bring our town back from the brink and thwart the conspiracy that had put our loved ones in the hospital. And with Gran at the helm, let's just say we were in for one bumpy ride!

CHAPTER 1

*V*esta had been jotting down a few random thoughts in her diary when she thought she heard a noise. She sat up a little straighter in bed—her favorite place to entrust her private musings to paper—and pricked up her ears. The sound seemed to come from the window, and as she slipped her feet from underneath the duvet—covered with drawings of orange cats as befits a self-confessed cat lady—she wondered if she shouldn't alert her son-in-law, no doubt still fast asleep in the room next to hers.

But then she decided against it. She prided herself on being a self-sufficient type of person who didn't need anything from anyone, and most definitely not from Tex, whom she had always considered something of an oaf. And so she tiptoed to the window, gripping her pen in her right hand as a weapon, hoping she wouldn't encounter a burglar or some other individual intent on perpetrating some nefarious designs on her person. If it was, she would give him or her the benefit of the sharp end of her pencil. After all, the pencil is still mightier than the sword.

When she arrived at the window, which was of the dormer variety, and looked out, she saw that the noise had originated from a large bird with black plumage, who seemed intent on hammering his way into the house by applying his sharp beak to the pane. If she wasn't mistaken, it was a raven—never a good sign!

She lowered the pencil and gave the bird a not-so-friendly look. "What do you want?" she asked in an irascible tone. If the bird understood what she was saying, it didn't give any indication, for it simply kept hammering away, as if its life depended on it. For a moment, she considered chasing it away, but then she had a better idea. Clearly, the bird was either laboring under a misapprehension that there was food to be had inside the house it was beleaguering with its presence, and it wasn't going to stop until it personally ascertained whether this was true or not, or it had some kind of urgent message to impart on its inhabitants.

So she tiptoed out of her room, barefoot across the wooden floor, and gently nudged open the door of her daughter and son-in-law's room. As she had surmised, two of their four cats were sound asleep at the foot of the bed. So she let out a noise like a steam whistle, causing all those resting in the bed to sit up with a jerk. She had intended to quietly whisper a word or two to the cats, but as usual, she didn't know the strength of her own voice.

The upshot was that both Tex and Marge were wide awake, and also Harriet and Brutus.

"There's a bird," she said in her defense. "I think it wants something. Could you..." She had addressed herself to Harriet and Brutus, but it was Marge who responded.

"Go back to bed, Ma," she said. And she immediately plunked down again to show her mother how it was done.

"Not... enough... sleep," Tex murmured as he followed his

wife's example. He smacked his lips for a moment, giving his mother-in-law a sleepy look, and promptly dozed off again.

Lucky for Vesta, Harriet and Brutus were made of sterner stuff, and after she had given them a gesture that told them all they needed to know, they obediently hopped down from the bed and followed her into her own room.

"That's the bird," she said, gesturing to the black raven, still pecking away to its dark heart's content. "So if you could please ask what it wants?"

"I'm not sure this is such a good idea, Gran," said Harriet. "Birds, as a rule, startle easily."

"She's right," said Brutus. "The moment we jump up onto that windowsill, it will simply fly off."

They were absolutely right, of course. Birds and cats will probably never really see eye to eye, owing to differing viewpoints on the nature of food. Cats consider birds an essential staple of their diet, while birds take an entirely different view.

"Just ask what it wants," she said, "without going anywhere near it." When her cats continued to stare at her, she clarified, "Just holler, will you?"

Harriet smiled. She had finally understood. And so she cleared her throat, opened those formidable pipes she had on her, and yelled, "Hey, bird! What do you want from us?!"

For the first time since it had landed on Vesta's windowsill, the bird downed tools and showed an interest in the inhabitants of the room it was trying to break into.

"Yeah, just tell us what it is you want," Brutus added his two cents, also hollering at the top of his lungs, which, like Harriet's, were quite formidable.

The bird now cocked its head, as birds often do, and prefaced any remarks it intended to make by giving Vesta the benefit of a lengthy stare. Then it finally gave them the benefit of the sound of its voice by declaring something that

Vesta didn't understand since she didn't speak the creature's language.

She turned to Harriet. "What did it say?"

"I think it wants you to open the window."

"But then it will fly away," said Vesta. "Won't it?"

Brutus shrugged. "I got the same message," he confessed.

And since a full quorum had given her the go-ahead, Vesta stalked over to the window and opened it. She shouldn't have been afraid the bird would take flight. Instead, it hopped onto the windowsill and glanced around the room. When its beady eyes landed on Harriet and Brutus, it seemed to puff out its chest and launched into a long harangue of words that came across as a lot of chirruping. When finally the stream of chirps dried up, Vesta saw that Harriet and Brutus sat looking up at the bird with looks of surprise etched on their furry faces.

"Well?" she asked. "What does it want? Tell me already!"

Brutus cleared his throat. "It says that…" He glanced uncertainly in Harriet's direction, but the Persian, contrary to her habit, seemed to have been struck dumb.

"What?" Vesta prompted. She was still holding on to her pencil, and if someone didn't start talking soon, she had a good mind to prod them with said pencil.

Finally, it was Harriet who spoke. She glanced up at Vesta with those remarkable green eyes of hers and said, "The bird wants you to cease and desist."

"Cease and desist? Cease and desist what?" She hated it when people spoke in riddles, and that applied to cats and birds, too.

"Cease and desist turning your backyard into a dead zone," said Brutus.

"And the front yard, too," said Harriet.

"I don't get it," she admitted. "My backyard isn't a dead zone. It's full of flowers and plants and all manner of greenery!" If there was anything she prided herself in, it was the fact that she possessed a green thumb.

"You use too many pesticides," Brutus said. "Causing all the worms to take a hike. And worms being a principal food source for birds, you're depriving this poor bird and all of its friends of sustenance."

The bird launched into a series of chirrups once more, with Harriet and Brutus listening intently. "It also says you have to convince your neighbors to stop using pesticides," said Harriet.

"But most importantly," said Brutus. "It wants you and that neighborhood watch of yours to stop the development of Blake's field."

Now *that* Vesta could understand. The field that ran behind her house—and all the houses of their neighbors—had, in recent years, been allowed to turn into a minor jungle, with weeds and all manner of life allowed to spring up in wild abandon, no doubt becoming a haven for the local bird population. But now that Blake Carrington had given the go-ahead for the piece of land to be sold off and put into development, it wouldn't be long before that was all a thing of the past, with devastating consequences for all the species that lived there.

"There isn't a lot I can do about that," she said. "Blake sold the land, and the new owner seems intent on getting rid of what he calls an eyesore." Most of their neighbors were glad that the field would finally yield to a more aesthetically pleasing development, and everyone was hoping for a nice set of condos that would considerably raise the value of their own properties.

"Clark says you have to stop the development," Harriet reiterated. "In fact, he says that you're his last hope."

Now this was more to Vesta's liking. She often got the impression that she was the only one who valued the existence of their neighborhood watch, but clearly there were others who thought the same thing—even if those others were of the feathered variety. "I'm afraid I don't know very much about it," she said. "All I know is that the field was sold off. I don't know anything about the new owner."

Brutus gave her a keen look. "So maybe it's time you found out, Gran?"

"After all, if they erect some tall building, it will make a big difference for all of us," Harriet argued. "Or imagine if they build a noisy factory? Or a wall?"

She shivered. The thought had occurred to her, but seeing as life had kept her pretty busy of late, she hadn't really looked into the sale of Blake's field yet. So she turned to the bird. "Clark, is it?"

The bird nodded. Or at least she thought it did.

"I'll look into the sale of the field," she said. "But I can't promise you that what I find will make you happy. And I can't promise that I'll be able to stop any development plans that might be harmful to your species."

"What about the pesticides, Gran?" asked Harriet. "You know you shouldn't use those. It's probably bad for us, too." She gave Vesta a reproachful look that spoke volumes.

"But I don't use pesticides!" she assured her audience. And even if she did, what harm could it do? All of it was approved by the EPA, as far as she knew. But as the bird kept giving her the evil eye and causing her to feel antsy, she finally caved. "Oh, fine," she said, throwing up her hands. "I'll see what I can do, all right?"

"And you will talk to the neighbors?" Brutus insisted.

"I will talk to the neighbors," she said. Though she didn't think they'd roll over and comply as easily as she just had. And all because of one stupid bird!

The bird chirped again, and Harriet smiled and said,

"Clark says thank you, and he will be following your future progress with considerable interest."

Somehow, and she didn't know why, she felt that there was more than a hint of menace in those words. But then she shrugged it off and gave the bird a quick nod. Clark seemed to return the nod and then spread his wings and flew off.

CHAPTER 2

Ronnie Vincent stared up at the ceiling and admired the brave and enterprising little spider that had attached itself to the corner of the molding. Lying next to his wife, he didn't stir, for fear of waking her up and causing her to turn over and pepper him with questions about his intentions, as she had done incessantly since he had told her the news. It wasn't that he didn't have the answers she was looking for, but more that he didn't want to get embroiled in another argument. After all, even though his intentions were pure, it was obvious that Lorie didn't exactly agree with him in that regard.

He should have known that when he launched this latest venture of his there would be pushback and plenty of wailing and gnashing of teeth. But he hadn't foreseen that it would be his own wife who would be most vocal amongst that crowd of naysayers and vehement critics of his work. He had tried to explain that he was doing it all for them—for the future of their family and most importantly for their kids, Sophie and Hannah. But it had all been for naught. Clearly Lorie had entirely different notions of what that future should look like, and it certainly didn't include the plans he had in mind.

He now placed his hands underneath his head and closed his eyes, as he gave himself up to thought. After all, it wasn't every day that you got the chance to change the world. To make it over in your own image. From scratch, as it were. As if yours was effectively the hand of God making tabula rasa and rummaging around with all creation. He grimaced. Lorie had accused him of harboring delusions of grandeur, and as he listened to his own thoughts, he wondered if she didn't have a point. To think he was God! Oh, the hubris!

The sleeping form of his wife stirred, and for a moment he held his breath. The last thing he needed was for another argument to ensue. He had enough on his plate as it was without trouble in the home adding to the list. But when her even breathing continued unabated, he soon relaxed. This was the moment that the tiny spider suddenly decided to take the great leap into the beyond and started abseiling from the ceiling, practically touching his face as it did. For a moment he fully thought it was going to land on his face and use it as a launch platform for further adventures. But as he watched the spider, his eyes going cross-eyed as he did, the spider must have become aware of the danger that lurked beneath and quickly reeled itself in and raced back up to the ceiling, where it was safe from harm and where no doubt it hoped to snatch a couple of fat flies as harbingers of great meals to come. Ronnie closed his eyes and dreamed of bigger things and the success of his venture, and soon he was fast asleep himself.

At least until a minor earthquake shook him to his foundations. When he opened his eyes, he saw that the earthquake consisted of their two daughters, Hannah and Sophie, and they were using his belly as a trampoline, as they often did. The noise they produced was enough to wake up an elephant, and since he and Lorie weren't denizens of that ancient and noble species, it didn't take them long to be fully awake. And as they gazed into each other's eyes while their offspring settled in between them, he wondered what his wife was thinking. For some reason, he had the impression she still wasn't very happy with him right now.

But that couldn't be helped. Whether she liked his plans or not, he was still going ahead with them.

The die was cast, and it was too late to put the genie back in the bottle.

BRENTON BROOKE DARTED a quick look left and right, then proceeded to cross the street at a trot, as was his habit. As a kid, his pop had always told him that traffic was a killer, and that you had to approach it like you did a wild beast of the jungle: by making sure you never allowed it to catch you unawares. And so he still made sure no car could ever come anywhere close to his person and run him over, as that particular species seemed to be in the habit of doing. A great big hulking monster of a vehicle honked its horn, and if he was startled, he didn't give any indication. He simply put more pep in his step and, not unlike a ballerina, performed a sort of pirouette in midair and made sure he was safely on the sidewalk before the vehicle could chew up parts of his person and maul him to death between its slathering jaws.

He gazed up at the facade of the building, and for a moment hesitated about whether he should set foot inside or not. But then he screwed up his courage to the sticking point and placed one foot on the threshold, a hand firmly on the knocker, and gave the implement a vigorous shake. Moments later, the sturdy door was yanked open by a liveried and bearded specimen that he surmised was some species of butler, so he stated his case. The underling listened without giving any indication that there was life behind the impassive facade but then deigned to step aside and allow him entry into the abyss. And so it was, with a beating heart and bated breath, that he placed himself into the hands of fate by entering the lair of Edmond Orbell, the eminent physician who came highly recommended by anyone dealing with the affliction that currently held him in its grip. After all, if Doctor Orbell couldn't see his way to returning him to full health, no one could.

Moments later, he was seated in the medical miracle worker's waiting room, where he found himself in the company of no fewer than three other patients, picked up a copy of Physician's Weekly from the salon table, and pretended to wait patiently for his turn. In actual fact, anxiety now held him firmly in its grip. And try as he might, he couldn't escape the notion that he may have made a mistake by placing his fate in the hands of Doctor Orbell.

One by one, the other inhabitants of the waiting room were called away by a friendly-looking nurse, and then finally, it was his turn. He rose from the plush and comfortable chair, replaced the copy of the medical journal on the table, and meekly followed the nurse down the corridor. She led him into the inner sanctum of Edmond Orbell's emporium and told him to take a seat while adding those time-honored words, "The doctor will see you soon," then silently closed the door.

Oddly enough, she hadn't even told him to take off all of his clothes, except for his socks and underwear. Not that he was upset about that, as he wasn't in the habit of taking off his clothes in the presence of ladies he had never met before. He might be a lot of things, but most of all he was a gentleman, and what was more, a gentleman who was faithful to his one true love, now more or less patiently sitting at home awaiting further proceedings. For he wasn't the only one who was anxious about what the day would bring.

Before long, the door opened and closed again, and as a man of voluminous aspect and dressed in a white smock strode in, a stethoscope dangling from his impressive neck, he knew he was in the presence of medical greatness.

"Mr... Brooke," he said, reading from the file he carried. And as he took a seat behind his desk, he gave him the benefit of a wintry smile. "So what can I do for you, Mr. Brooke?"

Which was his cue to turn from a normal human being into a blubbering mess of a man in just about two seconds flat, possibly setting a new world record.

CHAPTER 3

For some reason I couldn't quite comprehend, I found myself on the floor of the bedroom where I like to spend my nights. Under normal circumstances, I sleep at the foot of the bed that I share with my human Odelia and her husband Chase. Now though, try as I might, I couldn't remember how I had ended up on the floor next to the bed instead of in my usual spot. The only thing I could think was that Odelia must have had a nightmare and had kicked out with her feet, propelling me from the bed and landing my tush on the floor.

Lucky for me, Odelia has had the foresight of placing a small carpet next to the bed to protect her bare feet from the cold hardwood floor, and it was on this carpet that I now found myself, bemused and befuddled.

I glanced up at the bed, but nothing stirred, so whatever had caused me to fall from that great height, it was all in the past now. Even though I tried to search my memory, nothing presented itself as a possible explanation.

"You jumped down all by yourself, Max," suddenly a voice rang out not that far from me. When I glanced in the direction of the sound, I discovered that Grace, Odelia and Chase's little girl, was looking at me intently from the safety of her cot.

"I jumped down?" I asked.

"I saw you do it," said the blond-haired little angel as she studied her fingernails. "'Twas the middle of the night, and not a creature stirred when all of a sudden you uttered a strange sound and jumped from the bed."

"What sound?" I asked, intrigued by this story.

She frowned. "Eeek," she said. "If memory serves."

"Eeek?"

"That's right. It sounded as if you were having a nightmare. I remember thinking something must have scared you because knowing you, it takes a lot to elicit such a sound. So whatever you were dreaming of, it must have been pretty terrifying." She shivered. "Please tell me what it was, Max. Was it very horrible?"

It's a trait I've noticed in many a human person: this obsession with the macabre and the ghoulish. On the one hand, they profess to hate scary things, but on the other, they love it. It's a quirk I don't share with them, I have to admit. For me, scary is scary, and however you choose to look at it, it never becomes fun.

"I don't remember," I confessed. "I don't even remember how I ended up down here instead of up there."

"A nightmare," she said, nodding confidently. "And a very scary one."

A third voice now joined the conversation. It was my good friend and housemate Dooley, and as he stuck his head over the edge of the bed and gazed down into the precipice, he looked pretty scared himself, I have to say. "Was it very terrible, Max?" he asked. "This nightmare you had? What was it about? Were there monsters? Was there…" He shook violently. "Was there a giant spider?!"

"Like I just told Grace, I don't remember having a nightmare," I told my fluffy-haired feline friend. "All I know is that I woke up just now and found myself on the floor."

"On the rug," Grace corrected me. She always was a stickler for *le mot juste*.

"On the rug," I agreed, giving her the benefit of a grateful smile.

"Pity I can't look into your head," she said now. "And see what your nightmare was about."

Now it was my turn to shiver violently. Imagine if people started looking into your head and reading your mind. Now, wouldn't that be a most terrifying thing?

"I'm sure it was nothing," I told her. "Just one of those things, you know."

"Indigestion," said Dooley. "It often leads to bad dreams. What did you eat last night, Max? Was it something heavy? I'll bet that's what made you suffer that nightmare you had."

I didn't recall having eaten a heavy meal. Just a few nuggets of food as usual. As a rule, I don't like to eat before retiring for the night, since I hate falling asleep with a full stomach. But try as I might, I couldn't convince Dooley that his theory wasn't accurate. So finally I decided to drop it. The topic bored me already.

"I dreamed of my first day of school," said Grace, a beatific smile on her face now. "I can't wait to start school, you guys. Meet a lot of great friends. Meet the person who's going to take me by the hand and lead me to the world of grown-ups. Who will transfer all of her wisdom and knowledge to me and fill my head with wonder and the miracle of enlightenment. It's one of those watershed moments in any young person's life that I, for one, can't wait to launch into."

Dooley and I both stared at the kid. "That's… great," I said, a little lamely, I must admit. For some reason, I had a feeling that reality might not live up to the dream. Though of course it was entirely possible that she met such a wonderful teacher who would usher in a world of wonder, erudition, culture, and intellect. As it was, she was already a lot smarter than I was, even at her young age.

She now glanced out of the window, located next to her cot. Sunlight was starting to seep in, and as she took in the new dawn, she said, "You guys, something's going on in Blake's field."

"Yeah, rumor has it that the field has been sold," I told her. "So it looks like they'll be turning it into something other than a derelict piece of wasteland."

"Diggers have arrived," she said. "And if I'm not mistaken, they're going to start digging a very big hole any moment now."

Dooley and I shared another look, this time of alarm. "But I thought they were going to turn it into a park?" said my friend. "Do they need diggers to create a park, Max?"

"I'm sure they do," I said. "They need to get rid of all those weeds and bushes and the ramshackle structures that have sprung up over there. So diggers are probably the best way to go."

Dooley relaxed and placed his head on his paws. "I like parks. Parks are nice. Kids playing, people relaxing, birds chirping... Maybe we can even move cat choir to this new park. That way we don't have to walk so far at night."

"Yeah, that would be a good idea," I said. Though I wasn't sure our neighbors would necessarily agree. For some reason, humans don't often appreciate the artistic contribution a cat choir makes to the world of music.

And I would have closed my eyes for a quick little nap when suddenly Brutus and Harriet burst into the room. "You guys!" Harriet yelled. "They're going to turn Blake's field into a factory!"

"Or a wall!" said Brutus.

"Or an ugly office tower!"

Odelia, who had finally woken up from all the noise, muttered sleepily, "What's with all the racket?"

"The field, Odelia!" said Brutus. "Some developers are going to build the Empire State Building right next to our home—and we have to stop them!"

In a flash, I suddenly remembered what my nightmare had been about: for some reason, I had found myself falling into a deep, dark, bottomless pit!

CHAPTER 4

Tex Poole had a habit, developed over the course of the last couple of years, to venture out into his backyard first thing in the morning and potter about there for a while before getting ready for his day at the office. It supplied him with a certain measure of peace and generally contributed to his mental well-being. Being a doctor by profession, he encountered his fair share of challenges, and as he never stopped advising his patients, a healthy mind often leads to a healthy body. Or, in the words of an old professor of his, *mens sana in corpore sano*, or something along those lines.

And so when he stepped out of the house in his old rubber boots and his old jogging pants, en route to his trusty old garden house, he already was playing several scenarios in his head of how the start of his day would go. First, he'd deadhead a couple of those roses, and then make sure that chrysanthemum bush was fully devoid of pesky aphids, which had selected his garden as their hunting ground of late. As he traversed the short distance, he saw that he wasn't the only one out and about at this early hour. Next door, Ted

Trapper had the same idea he'd had and was also stomping about in his old galoshes, minding his patch of green delight.

Feeling in a particularly good mood, owing to a perfect night of uninterrupted sleep—not always an easy feat at his age—he shuffled over to the hedge that neatly divided his property from Ted's and addressed his neighbor. If he had expected Ted to return his hearty greeting in kind, he was sadly disappointed. Ted seemed reluctant to engage his neighbor in conversation, to the point that he appeared oddly withdrawn and even peevish to some extent. Being a naturally bonhomous person, Ted could never be fully cantankerous, but even so, he certainly wasn't his usual sunny self.

"What's wrong, Ted?" asked Tex, his keen medical eye already trying to ascertain symptoms of some possible disease—an occupational hazard with doctors.

"Nothing's wrong," said Ted testily as he kicked at the root of a nearby tree.

"Ted," said Tex. "It's me, Tex. You can tell me if something's the matter."

Ted glanced this way and that and finally relented. "Oh, all right. I don't mind telling you that I think it's all rotten. Rotten, Tex—rotten!"

Tex, somewhat taken aback by this sudden vehemence from one who was usually so placid and content with his lot in life, suppressed an urge to ask the man to open his mouth and say, 'Ahhh.' Instead, he simply nodded in what he hoped was a compassionate and encouraging fashion, which wasn't hard after twenty-five years on the job. "Please tell me all about it," he said.

And that's when the floodgates opened. Prefacing his remarks, Ted flapped his arms like a chicken for a moment, then cried, "We're being taken over, Ted! By some corporate giant. And who knows what they'll do to us. For all I know they'll close down the office and transfer me to some corporate headquarters on the other side of the country. And I don't mind telling you I don't like it. In fact, I hate it!"

Tex felt for the man. Many a person had entered his office six months or a year after having been submitted to exactly such a contingency and having developed an ulcer as a consequence, or, worse, some more deleterious disease. "My advice would be not to worry, Ted," he said, repeating the mantra he had used on all of those facing a similar fate. "And simply hope for the best. At least they're not letting you go. Are they?"

"No, they've assured us that our jobs are safe," Ted admitted reluctantly. "But they can't guarantee that we'll still be employed at our current location." He flapped his arms some more. "This is our home, Tex. This is where I raised my kids. This is where I grow my tomatoes. I don't want to move to Oregon."

"Is that where the new headquarters is?"

Ted nodded. "Some big giant corporation that's been hoovering up local businesses all over the country. If this keeps up, they'll become the number one accountancy firm in America, and we'll simply be one of their subdivisions."

"It's a tragedy," Tex said mournfully, though secretly he couldn't hide a frisson of pleasure at the notion that the Trappers might be moving soon. For some reason, Ted and he had never really seen eye to eye. On the other hand, who knew who might replace him. They might be off even worse than they were now. As the man said: you know what you have, but not what you might get instead. "Drop by the office later," he told his neighbor. "I'll give you something for the anxiety."

"Would you, Tex?" said Ted with such gratefulness that he felt guilty for harboring even a single bad thought about the man. "Would you really?"

"Of course. And try not to worry too much. It's bad for your ticker."

"You're right," he said. "Marcie tells me the same thing. But try as I might, I just can't stop thinking about what might happen if we do have to move. The girls live close by and drop by any time they can get away, and if we'll be halfway across the country, who knows how often we'll see them. And if we're ever blessed with grandkids, we might never see them—or only once or twice a year." He sighed deeply and reached out a hand across the hedge and pressed it to Tex's arm. "You're a lucky man, Tex, to have Odelia living right next door, and Grace. Very lucky."

Ted smiled. He knew his neighbor was right. Suddenly a window was thrown open upstairs, and Vesta yelled, "Tex! The bathroom is free, so you better get a move on while the water is still hot! On the double, soldier. Chop chop!" And then she closed the window with a bang, causing the pane to rattle in its frame.

Tex winced, and so did Ted.

"Okay, so maybe you're not that lucky," said Ted.

And that was probably the understatement of the year.

CHAPTER 5

Levi Kidner had been walking along the street for a while when he suddenly experienced a sort of wet sensation on the top of his head. As he reached a hand to the spot under consideration, he discovered that a gel-like substance had been deposited there. He retracted the hand and studied the substance for a moment with idle curiosity before, as anyone in his situation would, looking up to try and ascertain the source of the substance.

He had been walking along a wall of aged aspect, and above that wall several trees were visible, their limbs extending above his head. And on one of those limbs, a large bird of black plumage sat, looking at him with what could only be termed a hostile gaze. The bird now cocked its head and released another dropping, this time landing on his brow, before taking flight while uttering a raucous croak.

"It happened to me last week," said a man who passed him. "Exactly in this spot. And if I'm not mistaken, it was that very same bird."

"That bird pooped on me," said Levi, a sense of injury and

injustice making his voice wobbly. "It actually pooped on me. Twice!"

"It pooped on me, too," said the man, giving him a mournful look. "And on my best suit, no less. It's still at the cleaners. You're lucky," he added, pointing to Levi's head, "that it didn't poop on your suit."

It was true that Levi had stepped out of the house wearing his very best suit. He had a big meeting coming up, for which he felt it important to look his absolute best. Even in this day and age of Zoom calls and people dressing in their underwear to conduct their meetings, he was of the old-fashioned notion that it was important to dress well.

"Here," said the man, as he offered him a clean handkerchief. "Ever since this happened to me, I've been carrying one of these around. You never know when that bird might get it into its head to carry out another attack."

"But why?" asked Levi. "Why would it poop on perfectly innocent passersby?"

"Must be something wrong with it," said the man, who now introduced himself as Chris Griggs. "Sometimes birds will get like this."

"You're something of a bird aficionado, are you?" asked Levi as he passed the handkerchief across his scalp and forehead, thereby removing the avian detritus.

"Absolutely not," said Mr. Griggs with a shy smile. "Though I have to say that ever since the poop incident, I've been studying up on the species. Did you know, for instance, that birds are often considered harbingers of things to come?"

"Is that a fact?" asked Levi, not all that interested in the psychology of birds.

"It's true," Mr. Griggs assured him. "Whenever a disaster is afoot, birds know. Often before an earthquake or a storm, they will go a little crazy." He darted one eye at the sky in a foreboding sort of fashion. "So to be absolutely honest with you, the fact that this bird has gotten into the habit of pooping on people doesn't bode well. In fact, it doesn't bode well at all."

Levi thanked the man for sharing this remarkable insight, returned the soiled handkerchief, and went on his way. All this pop psychology was of no interest to him, and frankly smelled of the kind of stuff you read in magazines—horoscopes and such. And so by the time he had reached his destination, he had all but forgotten the incident. It came as something of a surprise, therefore, when he let himself into the office, and instead of finding his trusty secretary awaiting his arrival, he found a large policeman of foreboding aspect. It was unmistakable he was a policeman, for he was dressed in a policeman's uniform, conducted himself as a policeman, and even offered Levi the badge that proved his bona fides.

"What can I do for you?" he asked, even though what he would have liked to ask was, 'What have you done with my secretary?' Judging from the man's size, for a brief moment he wondered if he had devoured that trusty lady whole. He shouldn't have worried, though, for only a moment had passed before Mrs. Foxall came hurrying in, purse in hand and mink coat still on, apologizing profusely for being late. When her keen bespectacled eye landed on the policeman, for a moment she was as startled as Levi had been, but then she immediately proved her mettle by demanding in steely tones what the big idea was.

"I did ring the bell," the policeman, whose name was Randal Skip, said. "But when no one answered, I decided to let myself in. I hope you don't mind."

Levi exchanged a look with Mrs. Foxall. "The door was open?" asked the secretary.

"It was," Officer Skip assured them.

"But..." Mrs. Foxall frowned, causing the temperature in

the room to drop another few degrees. No one could do frosty as she could, which was one of the reasons he had hired her in the first place. A lawyer's office shouldn't project an atmosphere of gaiety and pleasant cheer. It should give the opposing counsel who is so bold to wander in, the feeling he's just been hit in the eye socket by the heavyweight champion of the world, and the unsuspecting client that he's going to be taken seriously before being relieved of a substantial sum of money. "But I locked the door last night," she said. "I know I did."

Levi also knew this. Mrs. Foxall was nothing if not the consummate professional. Blessed with a mind like a steel trap, her discerning eye missed nothing.

"The door was open," Officer Skip insisted stubbornly.

Which is when Levi realized that something was rotten in the state of Denmark. Or rather his office. He wasn't a man prone to flights of fancy or feats of athleticism, but the alacrity with which he left his secretary's office was akin to that of Usain Bolt hoping to snatch another gold medal. Moments later he was standing in his office overseeing the devastation. And if he hadn't clutched at his head when that bird had elected to use it for target practice, he did so now. For as he looked around, the mess that met his eye hurt his very core. A fastidious dresser, as has already been established, this trait extended throughout both his personal and professional life in a general sense of tidiness and appreciation for order. But as he looked around, all he saw was disorder, as if a hurricane had hit his office and decided to wreak havoc.

"What happened here!" Mrs. Foxall cried as she joined him at the door.

"Burglars," said the cop, giving them the benefit of his professional opinion. He darted a keen-eyed look at the lawyer. "You, sir, have been burgled!"

CHAPTER 6

Chase hadn't slept well, which wasn't like him. Usually, he only had to lie down and he was fast asleep the moment his head hit the pillow. These last couple of days, though, he'd taken to tossing and turning all night, before finally falling asleep in the early morning hours, at which point his alarm clock went off the moment he fell asleep. Or at least that's how it felt. Odelia, too, was having a hard time finding sleep lately, and now he wondered if it might have something to do with the house or the bed. Maybe there was some kind of problem they needed to tackle. Which is why the moment he got out of bed, he immediately started examining the bedroom, trying to get at the root cause of their sleep issues.

"What are you doing?" asked Odelia as she observed this strange behavior.

"I'm trying to figure out what's been troubling us," he explained. "It's probably something to do with the bed, don't you think? Maybe we need a new mattress?"

Odelia had been conversing with her cats again, as was her habit, and judging from the way those creatures had been meowing up a storm, they, too, were facing some little difficulty of their own. What that was, he had no idea, since he didn't possess the same gift as his wife did—or their daughter Grace, for that matter.

"Or it could be the pillow," he said as he picked up his own specimen and subjected it to a closer scrutiny. "They say that you need to change these things every couple of years. How old is this one, you think?"

"It's not the pillow," said Odelia. "Or the mattress. It's Blake's field. Someone bought it and now they're turning it into an office tower. Or a wall or something."

"A mall?"

"A wall."

He gave his wife a puzzled look. "Now why would they put a wall behind the house? That doesn't make sense."

Odelia shrugged. "A bird told my grandmother this morning that they're going to put up some kind of structure and asked her to stop the project."

This made even less sense. "A little birdie told your grandmother they're building something on Blake's field and she has to stop it?"

"By all accounts, it wasn't a little bird," said Odelia, stretching before getting up. "It was a big black bird. Possibly a crow or a raven or something. Anyway, the diggers have arrived, so they're definitely building something. But first they'll dig a hole. Well, you know how it goes." She was gazing out of their bedroom window now, and so he joined her. And much to his surprise, she was right: workmen were busily demarcating sections of Blake's field with wooden poles and string, and a line of diggers stood at attention, ready to start… digging, he assumed, for that's what diggers did. At least in his limited experience.

"Blake sold his field?" he asked.

"Didn't I tell you? I mean, let's face it. Considering he'll probably be old and gray by the time he's finished serving his sentence, he has no need for this plot of land. And since he doesn't have any heirs, he probably figured he might as well sell it."

"Yeah, but why sell it to a developer? Who knows what they'll build."

"I don't know, babe. I guess he didn't think we were in the market for a piece of land? Or maybe he wanted to thumb his nose at us for landing him in prison?"

It was certainly possible. After having arrested Blake, the man had indeed shown a certain rancor for the fate that Chase had relegated him to. Though he only had himself to blame, of course.

"I hope they won't put up an office tower. It will take away all of our sun. We'll perpetually be in the dark if that happens. Not to mention we'll have those apartments overlooking the backyard, taking away any notion of privacy."

"They can't put up an office tower," said Odelia. "This is a residential area. Office towers aren't allowed." She turned to her husband. "Are they?"

He wasn't an expert on zoning laws, but he was inclined to agree with her. "We should probably ask Charlene. She would have had to give the go-ahead."

That was one advantage to having a mayor in the family: you could always ask her about things like that.

Odelia visibly relaxed. "Charlene would never give her permission to put up an office tower in our backyard. No, I'm sure that bird was mistaken."

He smiled as he placed an arm around her shoulder, then pecked a kiss on her temple. "You wanna hit the shower or shall I go first?"

"You go first," she said magnanimously. "While I finish talking to the cats." She raised an eyebrow. "They're very upset about the prospect of Blake's field being developed, as you can probably imagine."

He grinned and left the bedroom to take a shower. Taking care of cats was akin to being a crisis manager: there was always some fire to put out, as Odelia's cats were of the highly-strung variety, frequently up in arms about something —or anything. He was happy that he didn't have to bother with all of that. Then again, he hadn't been born with the gift Odelia and her mom and grandma possessed.

As he was about to step into the shower, suddenly he became aware that he was not alone. A bird of black plumage had flown in through the window, which had been ajar to let some air in. The bird sat perched on the top of the shower cabin, and as he greeted it with a hearty 'Hey there, my feathered friend,' suddenly the bird released a sort of squawk, raised its wings, and pooped on top of his head!

"Hey!" he said, much surprised. "What did you go and do that for!"

But of course, the bird didn't respond. Instead, it emitted another few squawks and sailed out through the window.

He could be mistaken, but those squawks sounded a lot like riotous laughter!

CHAPTER 7

It wasn't easy for Odelia to calm us down, which clearly she felt was her main task, for the simple reason that obviously something was going on, even if she didn't want to admit it.

"Those diggers are there for a reason," said Harriet. "They're there to dig the foundations for that office tower. Before you know it, we're looking at a gigantic building that will change the quality of our lives forever."

"Or they could turn it into a park," said Dooley, who opted to take the charitable view. "And we could move cat choir to this new park, cutting down on our commute."

We all smiled at this. "It's not a commute if you're not actually commuting, Dooley," said Brutus. "And the trip to the park is, what, a couple of minutes?"

"It would still be a lot easier if the park came to us, instead of us having to go to the park," Dooley argued. "Like the mountain coming to Moses?"

"I don't think it was Moses," said Odelia. "But let's not get into all of that. I'm sure there's a perfectly good reason those diggers are there, and the moment I arrive at the office I'll ask Charlene about it—how does that sound?"

"It sounds like it will be too late!" said Harriet. "By the time you come home tonight, that office block will be up—and try tearing it down then!"

"Office blocks aren't built in a day, Harriet," said Odelia. "It takes months. And besides, Charlene would never give permission to build such a monstrosity in the middle of a residential area. There are rules and regulations. Building permits that need to be granted. So I'm sure whatever they're building, it's not an office block."

"Just you wait and see," said Harriet, not to be placated. "Clark told us to stop that development, so obviously Clark knows something we don't."

Odelia frowned. "Who's Clark?"

Harriet rolled her eyes. "Haven't you heard anything we said? The bird, Odelia—the bird!"

Odelia stiffened to some extent. She clearly didn't like to be spoken to in such a tone. "I said I'll speak to Charlene and I will. Now if we can all calm down?"

But Harriet wasn't the kind of cat you told to calm down. It only made her even more upset. "If you won't stop this development, we will," she said. "Us and the neighborhood watch." She raised her chin and her tail both. "Just you wait and see!" And with these words, she flounced out of the room.

Odelia muttered a silent oath. "You guys can see reason, right?" she asked. "Nobody will erect an office block behind our homes. They simply won't." But I had to say she didn't seem as sure of herself as she had been before.

"I don't know anything about this permit business," I told her. "All I know is what Clark said. So it's probably a good idea to look into this a little deeper."

"And I will!" said Odelia.

"Mom, your face is red," said Grace, who had been studying her parent closely. She was right, and so I felt that we had all said what we wanted to say, and now it was time to let things rest for a while. Odelia would talk to the mayor, and we would take a closer look at this development, and maybe glean some more information on our own. So we let Odelia pick Grace from her crib and get ready for their day while we got ready for ours.

As we slipped out through the pet door, Dooley asked, "Do you think Harriet is right, Max? Are they going to build some monstrosity behind the house?"

"I don't know, Dooley," I confessed. "But if they are, we probably would have heard about it, seeing as Charlene is the mayor, and we see her all the time."

"Maybe it's one of those illegal construction sites," said Brutus. "It happens, you know. They simply start building some illegal structure without asking permission first. And by the time the council gets wise, the building is done, and people have moved in, and they decide to let bygones be bygones, figuring it's too much of a hassle to deal with a bunch of disgruntled new homeowners."

"We won't let it get that far," I assured our friend. And as we went in search of Harriet, we found her on top of the fence, looking out across Blake's field and trying to determine what was going on there.

We joined her, and so moments later the four of us were all perched on the fence. What we saw wasn't of a nature to assuage our qualms. Quite the contrary. We saw men in hard hats traipsing about, shouting things to one another and looking very serious and very busy. We saw a man in a suit looking at a map and talking to another man in a suit, both gesticulating wildly and also wearing hard hats. And we saw men stomping about, measuring things and planting sticks. All in all, it didn't look as if they were doing this just for the heck of it. More like they had a plan, and that plan just might not suit our own plans for Blake's field.

"I hope it'll be a park," said Dooley, but he sounded a lot less sure of himself already.

"It's an office block," said Harriet. "I can feel it in my gut. And my gut never lies."

"It could be a row of houses," I suggested. "That would be more appropriate, since this whole neighborhood consists of houses."

"Whatever it is," said Brutus. "I don't like it. What's going to happen to those poor mice and those shrews? And all of those other species that live here?"

Now that was something I hadn't even taken into consideration. But Brutus was right. Over the course of the past couple of decades, Blake's field had become home to many different species. And judging from the way these men in hard hats were moving about the area, I had a feeling they didn't have these species' best interests in mind.

Suddenly, a bird joined us on the fence. It was Clark, the same bird who had offered such a stark warning that morning.

"Stop this nonsense before it's too late," he said now.

"What are they building?" asked Dooley. "Is it a park?"

Clark gave Dooley a critical look. "You're naive, aren't you?"

"No, I'm Dooley," said Dooley. "Naive must be some other cat."

Clark didn't even crack a smile. Obviously, he was a tough sort of bird. "Parks don't put money in the shareholders' pockets, Dooley," he said.

"They don't? Gee, I had no idea," said our friend.

"So what are they going to put up?" asked Harriet. "It's an

office block, isn't it? Tell me I'm right, Clark. A big monstrous office block that will obscure the sky."

"You don't know the half of it," said Clark. And with these mysterious words, he took off, leaving us to wonder what he possibly could have meant by that.

CHAPTER 8

Marge wasn't feeling too well. While her husband and her mother were already up and about, she was still in bed and felt like staying there for the rest of the day. She hadn't wanted to tell Tex because he would only worry about her, but as she now tried to slip her feet from under the covers, she immediately felt so dizzy she had to lie down again.

"Oh, dear," she said as she gripped her brow and closed her eyes again. The whole room seemed to be turning on its axis, as if someone had given the world a spin, and it was whirling like a merry-go-round, with her hanging on for dear life.

Just then, the bedroom door burst open, and Tex walked in. "You'll never believe what I've just heard," he said.

"Mh?" she said, with a lot less enthusiasm than her husband's statement warranted.

"It's the Trappers," he said, a sort of triumphant note in his voice. "They're moving away! The company Ted works for has been gobbled up by some corporate giant, and they're closing down their local branch and making all of its personnel move to headquarters. In Oregon!"

"You don't have to sound so jolly about it," she said. "Poor Ted. Poor Marcie."

"Yeah, poor Ted and Marcie," Tex echoed as he took a seat on the bed. She felt his eyes on her, and she made a concerted effort to open hers. "You don't look well, honey," said her husband, the doctor. "Is it your head?"

She shook the instrument in question. "It's everything," she admitted, seeing no sense in delaying the inevitable. That was the trouble when you married a doctor: you could never keep anything from him. On the other hand, it was also a blessing, of course. "I feel rotten, Tex. Rotten all over."

Immediately his frown of concern morphed into a kind of practical display of professional interest. And as he launched into a series of questions and quickly checked her pulse, it wasn't long before he came to a conclusion. "We need to get you to a hospital—pronto."

"I'm sure there's no need for that," she protested feebly. The last thing she wanted was to go to the hospital. She hated hospitals. They stuck needles into you in odd places, made you wear funny clothes, and the whole procedure led to no end of trouble before they decided they were finally through with you.

"No buts," he said gently as he held on to her hand. "It could be an innocent bug you caught, but it could also be the harbinger of something much more dangerous. And I, for one, don't want to take any chances—do you?"

"I guess not," she admitted. She sighed. "The trouble is that the moment I try to stand, the whole room starts turning cartwheels."

"I'll help you get dressed and into the car," he suggested. "Or I could call an ambulance?"

"No ambulance," she hastened to say. The last thing she

needed was for an ambulance to alert the entire neighborhood that she was suffering from some malaise. "If you can drive me, I'm sure I'll make it to the hospital in one piece."

"Let's get you ready," he said, and gently assisted her out of bed and into some clothes. While she patiently sat at the edge of the bed, her eyes firmly closed, he packed an overnight bag, 'just in case,' and moments later he was assisting her down the stairs. It wasn't easy because she was dizzy as can be, but they finally made it into the car. As they drove away, she wondered briefly when she'd be back. In about an hour or so, she thought. As soon as all the examinations were done, and they concluded that she had indeed caught an innocent bug and would have to stay in bed for a couple of days—two at the most.

The hospital was its usual frenzy of people coming and going, ambulances driving to and fro, and generally not exactly conducive to one's feeling of well-being. "Don't leave me, Tex," she said as she gripped her husband's arm.

"Of course not," said Tex as he gave her a look of reassurance. "Are you kidding me? I'll be with you every step of the way, honey."

She smiled a weak smile. Her husband might be a doofus sometimes, but he was a good man and a good doctor.

"Are you ready?"

She nodded. "As ready as I'll ever be."

And so he helped her out of the car and into the wheelchair he'd secured from hospital reception. She had protested that she didn't need a wheelchair, but once she was in it, and they were traversing the parking lot, she had to admit she would never have been able to navigate the distance under her own steam, even with Tex supporting her. By the time they reached the hospital, she was feeling so weak she almost tumbled out of that wheelchair. That's when she realized that maybe she wouldn't be home today—or any of the coming days—or weeks.

As she glanced around, she saw that they were surrounded by dozens of other people, many whose faces were familiar to her, and all of them looking as weak and nauseous as she was feeling right then.

"My God," said Tex. "It's an epidemic!"

But then she did almost fall out of that wheelchair, and the next thing she knew, strong hands were expertly placing her on a stretcher, and she was being wheeled away. She searched around for a sign of her husband, and when she saw his face hovering over her, she gripped his hand for a moment before finally passing out.

"Hang in there, Marge," he was saying, his voice coming from far away.

CHAPTER 9

Odelia felt it was time to get some answers. So the first thing she did when she arrived at the office was pick up the phone and put in a call to the mayor, who also happened to be her uncle's wife. Oddly enough, she couldn't get through to Charlene's private number, and when she tried Town Hall, Charlene's secretary told her the mayor wouldn't be coming in today because she wasn't feeling well.

"Nothing serious, I hope?" she asked.

"She didn't sound great," said Imelda, who had been the mayor's personal secretary ever since Charlene had taken up the position. "I'm going to drop round later today with some flowers and a box of pralines."

Odelia hesitated, then decided to charge right ahead. From long association with Imelda, she knew that the woman knew as much or sometimes even more than Charlene herself about matters that concerned Hampton Cove. "You wouldn't know what they're building behind my house, would you, Imelda? It's just that we haven't been informed about any new construction going on."

"I don't know much about it," said Imelda cautiously. "Just

that Blake Carrington sold the land and an investment company snapped it up."

"So you have no idea what they're planning to do with that land?"

"I'm afraid you'll have to ask Charlene. All I know is that the land was sold to an investment company which has connections to a well-known university."

"What university would this be?"

"I'm sorry, but I have no idea."

"Okay, thanks, Imelda," she said. And since Charlene wasn't picking up her phone, she tried her uncle instead.

"Yes," her uncle's gruff voice boomed in her ear.

"Hey, Uncle Alec. I heard that Charlene isn't feeling well? Nothing serious, I hope?"

For a moment, her uncle didn't speak, then he heaved a sort of prolonged sigh. "She's feeling dizzy. Nauseous, you know. I'm sure it's just a bug, but just to be on the safe side, I was thinking about calling your dad. Only he's not picking up."

"Dad isn't picking up? That's odd."

"Yeah, it is."

She heard the sound of Charlene's voice in the background and understood that her uncle hadn't left for the office yet but had elected to stay home with his wife. That told her that Charlene might be in worse condition than she was letting on.

"Why don't you call another doctor?" she suggested.

"I would, but she won't let me," said her uncle darkly.

"I don't need a doctor!" she heard Charlene shout in the background. "I feel fine!"

"You don't look fine," her uncle said sternly. "You look terrible, honey."

"Gee, thanks for the compliment," Charlene quipped, but her heart wasn't in it, Odelia could hear.

"I'll try to reach my dad," Odelia promised. She would have broached the topic of the development, but clearly now wasn't the time, so she decided to drop it. Moments later, she had her dad on the phone. He sounded harried, and it didn't take her long to discover why that was.

"Your mother is in the hospital," he announced. "They won't tell me what she's got, but it looks a lot more serious than we thought at first. And the weird thing is that a lot of other people are being brought in, all suffering the same symptoms."

"And what are those?" she asked, concern making her grip her phone a little tighter.

"Nausea, dizziness, and a general sense of malaise before passing out."

"Sounds a lot like a virus to me," she said.

"I agree. Oh, honey, I hope she'll be all right."

The concern in her dad's voice made her experience a twinge of alarm, which she immediately tried to tamp down on. "I'm sure she'll be fine, Dad."

Now was not the time for her dad to pay house calls, so she merely mentioned that Charlene was suffering the same symptoms, and he advised her to go to the hospital immediately. "Until we know what we're dealing with, we shouldn't take any chances."

When she relayed that urgent message to her uncle, he sounded relieved.

"See?" he said, addressing his stubborn wife. "I told you."

"Oh, fine," said the mayor. "But I'm going under protest."

Odelia smiled. "Protest or not, better drive her down there right now."

"I will," said her uncle. "How is my sister?"

"I'm not sure. They won't tell Dad what she has."

For a moment, the big burly police chief was silent, then he said, "That doesn't sound good."

No, it sure didn't. Which is why she told her uncle she would meet him at the hospital, so she could look in on her mother personally.

Her next call was to her grandmother, to inform her of what was going on. Gran didn't seem overly concerned. She did ask her if she had discovered what was going on with Blake's field already, to which she had to admit she hadn't.

"It's all connected," the old lady said mysteriously. "Mark my words!"

Odelia's next call was to her husband, and Chase picked up on the first ring with the words, "It's a disaster. Half the force has taken ill! What's going on?"

"I'm not sure," she said, and told him about her mom and about Charlene and the strange symptoms they were both suffering from.

"Same here," said Chase. "Let's meet at the hospital."

"I don't like this, Chase," she said. "What's going on?"

"Beats me. But if it's a virus, we might all be coming down with this thing."

She certainly hoped not. The last thing she needed was to be taken ill. Then she remembered that Dan hadn't come into the office that morning. And so after promising her husband she'd meet him in front of the hospital, she called her boss. It took a while, and when the aged editor finally picked up, his voice sounded so weak she had trouble understanding what he was saying. "What was that, Dan?"

"I said..." He cleared his voice with difficulty. "I'm not feeling so great."

"Call an ambulance," she said immediately. "You've caught a virus."

He laughed a weak laugh. "I'm sure it's nothing as serious as that."

But when she told him about her mom and Charlene and what Chase had just told her, the editor became more animated. "Go down to the hospital right now and find out what's going on," he advised. "This could be the scoop of the century! Hampton Cove could be ground zero for a new epidemic!"

Oh, dear. Even when he was bedridden, he was still the editor.

"I will, Dan. But only if you call an ambulance right now. And if you won't, I will. Is that understood?"

"Perfectly," he said, sounding a lot better already. "But only if you get this scoop for the Gazette, Odelia! I want this story on the website ASAP!"

CHAPTER 10

"Where is everyone?" asked Gran. She had joined us by the fence, and even though she wasn't tall enough to look over it, judging from the noise the workers were making, it wasn't hard for her to fathom that something was going on back there.

"No idea," I said. "Probably at work."

"Marge and Tex are at the hospital," she now announced. "Apparently Marge came down with the flu."

We glanced back at the old lady. "Must be a bad case of the flu," I ventured, "if Tex took her to the hospital."

Gran shrugged. "You know what doctors are like. They panic at the least little sign of trouble. I'm sure she'll be just fine. So what are you guys up to?"

"Worrying," said Brutus somberly.

Gran laughed. "I thought it was only us humans who liked to worry. What are you worrying about?"

"Well, that thing Clark told us," said Harriet. "About the development of Blake's field?"

Gran made a throwaway gesture with her hand. "Nothing

to worry about. Just a lot of hullabaloo over nothing. Mountain and molehill and all of that jazz."

"But Clark said—"

"Clark is a bird!" Gran reminded us as if we needed the reminder. "Birds have very tiny brains. In fact, their brains are probably no bigger than a peanut. So I wouldn't listen to a word that worrier told us." She rubbed her hands. "Now that Tex is at the hospital, looks like I've got a whole day to fill with plenty of fun and pleasant activities. So what do you want to do first? Maybe play some games?"

We stared at her in abject dismay, and some of that dismay must have penetrated her own brain, possibly no bigger than a coconut by the looks of things.

"Oh, don't be like that, you guys," said Gran. "Everything is fine!"

"It doesn't look fine from where we are sitting," said Harriet and gestured with her tail in the direction of what used to be Blake's field.

"Odelia told me it's something to do with a university," Gran announced. "She talked to Charlene's secretary, Imelda, and seeing as that woman is the biggest gossip in all of Hampton Cove—along with her good friend Dolores—I'm guessing she's probably right."

"A university?" asked Harriet. "What does that mean?"

"Probably something to do with their agricultural department," Gran ventured a guess. "Maybe they'll examine the number of greenflies per square inch or something. They love that sort of thing. Okay, let's go and have some fun!"

I didn't feel like having fun, and neither did my friends, but if what Gran was saying was true, and Blake's field had been snapped up by a university, at least that dispelled some of our worst fears. Maybe she was right, and they were simply going to use the field as a laboratory to examine certain species that flocked there.

And so we hopped down from the fence and decided to humor our human.

"What do you want to do first?" asked Gran as she sat cross-legged on the lawn.

"Maybe we'll play catch," Brutus suggested. "You try to catch us, and we try not to be caught." He gave me a wink, and I could see what he was getting at. He'd simply disappear and take a prolonged nap, and by the time Gran was exhausted from the search, all this 'fun and games' business would be mercifully over.

I liked his way of thinking since I'm not a big fan of playing games myself. That's dogs, an entirely different species, with brains possibly even smaller than a peanut but a zest for chasing a ball that is unparalleled in the animal kingdom.

Just then, a plane flew by overhead, and as it did, a sudden rain shower soaked us to the skin.

"Yikes!" said Harriet, whose lustrous fur is her pride and joy.

"Where did that come from?" asked Gran irately as she patted her now wet tresses. She glanced up at the sky, which was as bright and sunny as always, not a cloud in sight. The plane continued on its trek across the firmament, and as the sound of its rotors died away, we all ventured indoors, where Gran proceeded to towel us dry, before applying a towel to herself as well. When her phone chimed, she decided to ignore it, probably figuring she had earned herself a vacation day and wouldn't be disturbed. But then the caller tried again —and again.

I checked the display and saw that Odelia was trying to reach her.

"It's Odelia," I told Gran.

And so finally she picked up. "What do you want?" she grumbled. She listened for a moment, then frowned. "It's the flu, honey. Nothing to worry about." But after Odelia continued to pour more words into her grandmother's ear, a niggle of concern made the old lady wince. "Are you sure about that? Yeah, of course I'll take care of the cats. Don't you worry about a thing."

After she hung up, she stared into space for a couple of seconds.

"What's going on?" asked Harriet, a note of panic in her voice.

Gran looked up. "Mh? Oh, that was Odelia. She's sick. Just like Marge. And Charlene, and Alec, and Chase—and Tex. And a lot of other folks." She produced an unconvincing laugh. "Looks like we're the only ones still standing, you guys!"

CHAPTER 11

When we arrived at the hospital to pay a visit to our family, we landed in what could only be described as pandemonium. Cars were parked haphazardly, blocking surrounding streets, since the parking lot itself was at capacity, and the same applied to the hospital itself, which was so full of patients they had to place them in the corridors. All of them seemed to be experiencing the same symptoms: a sense of nausea and dizziness followed by a deep coma from which they refused to wake up. Such was the case with Odelia when we finally found the room she was in. As it was, she was sharing her room with Chase, Charlene, Uncle Alec, Tex, and Marge, which was convenient since we didn't have to look for them.

"Oh, this is just too horrible," said Gran, who looked stricken, for possibly the first time since we had made that iron-willed old lady's acquaintance many moons ago. "I'm an orphan, can you believe it? At my age! An orphan!"

I could have told her that an orphan is a child whose parents have passed away, which at this instance wasn't exactly the case, but she was so distraught she wasn't susceptible to reason.

"Are they all going to die, Max?" asked Dooley.

"I'm sure they'll be fine, Dooley," I said, though I have to say I wasn't all that confident about their prospects myself.

"Are they asleep?" asked Harriet, who hadn't fully cottoned on to what was happening.

And I had to admit that they looked as if they were sound asleep. They all looked so peaceful and relaxed. Though they also had a certain waxlike complexion that I didn't like to see. When asleep, humans look more or less rosy-cheeked when they're in full health. And that definitely was not the case now.

A doctor walked in, wearing a look of grave concern on his face. Immediately Gran clutched at his arm. "Tell me what's wrong with them, doc."

The doctor carefully removed Gran's grip from his sleeve and gave her a look of compassion that didn't become him. Clearly, he wasn't used to it. "The problem is that we don't know what's ailing them yet, Mrs…"

"Muffin," said Gran. "Vesta Muffin. That's my daughter Marge over there, and that's my son Alec and my granddaughter Odelia. The rest…" She shrugged. "In-laws." She spoke the word with a certain harshness, as if she personally blamed Tex, Chase, and Charlene for putting their significant others in this state.

"We're doing everything we can, Mrs. Muffin," the doctor assured her. "But as you can probably see, we're currently being overrun, with a lot of patients being brought in, all suffering from the same mysterious malady." He studied her closely. "How are you feeling yourself?"

"Fine," Gran assured the doctor. "Fit as a fiddle, in fact. Never felt better."

"Peculiar," said the doctor as he stroked his chin. "And

you live in the same home with these relatives of yours? Eat the same food? Drink the same water?"

"Yep, absolutely. Though I should probably say I graciously allow *them* to live under *my* roof. I'm that kind of person, you see. Kind-hearted and altruistic."

"Most interesting," he said. "Do you mind?" He held up a device that looked entirely suspicious to me and reminded me of Vena Aleman, the vet.

"Of course, go right ahead," said Gran.

He then lifted the device to Gran's eyes and shone a light in them as he peered through the device.

"Most fascinating," the doc murmured. "Most fascinating indeed." He had grabbed hold of Gran's hand and was checking his watch as he fingered her wrist. To top it all off, he asked her to open her mouth and proceeded to study her tonsils. "Very interesting," he said in conclusion.

Gran smiled. "Is that what you say to all the girls, doc?"

The doctor didn't smile. "You're in excellent fettle, Mrs. Muffin."

"I know. That's what I just told you," she reminded him.

"I mean you don't seem to display any of the symptoms that your other family members suffer from. In spite of the fact that you live under the same roof, eat the same food, drink the same water, and, I presume, use the same bathroom?"

She gave him a nasty look. "What's that supposed to mean!"

The doctor smiled an appeasing smile and held up his hands. "My theory is that this virus—for we seem to be dealing with a mysterious new virus—is of the airborne variety. Which means it's being transferred from person to person through the air. But you don't seem to have caught it. Or maybe you're immune, who knows. Is it all right if I take a sample of your blood?"

Gran gave him a look of suspicion. Clearly, no man had ever asked her this before. "What are you, a vampire?"

"It would help determine what's causing this disease," he explained.

She thought for a moment, then relented. "Oh, all right. If you must." Moments later, we were in a nurse's station, and Gran had a rubber band strapped to her arm while a nurse was drawing blood. "I'm not the kind of girl who gives blood on her first date," she explained to the stoic-looking nurse. "But I'm willing to make an exception this one time."

Next to me, Dooley looked extremely unwell, and even Brutus and Harriet were showing all the hallmarks of this strange new disease that was wreaking havoc on Hampton Cove's population. The moment we stepped out into the corridor, they immediately recovered.

"It's the sight of blood," Harriet confessed. "It makes my knees wobble."

"Same here," Brutus admitted.

"Why are they punching holes in Gran and allowing her blood to leak out into those funny little tubes?" asked Dooley, who seemed to be the most affected of the four of us.

"Of all her family members, Gran is the only one who isn't in a coma right now," I explained. "So the doctor wants to know why she's not affected by this new virus. And he hopes to find the key to the mystery in her blood."

"I don't think it's fair," said Dooley. "She's the only healthy one, and she's being subjected to all kinds of tests. It should be the other way around."

"Oh, I'm sure they're testing everyone," I assured our friend.

"And besides, *we're* not sick, are we? So why aren't they checking *our* blood?" But then he realized what he was saying and quickly retracted his words. "Forget I said that. I don't want them to poke holes in me as well! I need my blood!"

"Nobody will poke any holes in you," I said.

"Are you sure, Max?" asked Brutus. "Ever heard the term 'guinea pig?'"

I gulped a little. Brutus was right. If they were going to start testing a possible remedy for this strange malady, they might start by testing it on us!

Which is why we decided to make ourselves scarce for now, but not before telling Gran that she could find us outside if she needed us, which she told us she did, for she had a plan. And not just *a* plan—*the* plan!

Uh-oh. Where had we heard that before?

CHAPTER 12

Levi Kidner wasn't feeling entirely at ease as he traversed the streets of his town. After the break-in that morning, the policeman on duty had told him that one of the neighbors had seen a person gain access to his office and had called it in, which is why the police were there waiting for him and Mrs. Foxall when they arrived. As far as he could tell, not a lot had been stolen, but what had been stolen was certainly cause for great concern. And so he had immediately told Mrs. Foxall to bring all of the documents relating to the same client to the bank and lock them up in their vault until further notice. Though most likely the damage was done.

The streets were eerily deserted, which was to be expected if the rumors about some disease sweeping through town were to be believed. Most of the shops were closed, and there were practically no people out and about. Though when he arrived at the General Store, he saw that Wilbur Vickery was still at his post as usual. Levi sighed a breath of relief. So at least some shops were still open, and some people had been spared. He entered the store and found

Vickery deep in conversation with an old lady he didn't recognize. The moment he walked in, the conversation halted, and they gave him a look of suspicion. But as he held up his hand in greeting, Vickery returned this greeting from a loyal customer in kind, and the twosome resumed their whispered conversation. No doubt gossiping about the tragedy that had befallen Hampton Cove.

He placed a few choice items in his basket and lined up at the checkout counter. Odd, he felt, that some people seemed to have been spared from contracting the disease, while others had fallen ill almost immediately. If the stories were true, hundreds or possibly even thousands of people were in a coma and had been transferred to different hospitals since their own local hospital couldn't handle the workload. As he patiently waited for his turn to place his items on the conveyor belt, his phone vibrated, and he quickly took it out. When he saw who it was that was trying to reach him, he stiffened with apprehension.

'Let this be a warning,' the message read.

A chill danced the tango up and down his spine, and he wondered if his own life wasn't in danger of being snuffed out. But then he figured he was probably too important to the organization to be dealt with in such an unceremonious fashion.

Still, it behooved him to be more careful from now on. You never knew.

By the time it was his turn to pay for his wares, his thoughts were already spinning different scenarios for getting out of Hampton Cove. Maybe it was time to close up shop and shake the dust of this town off his well-shod feet.

When he walked out of the General Store and glanced around, it was with a distinct sense of regret. "Sayonara," he murmured quietly. "And my apologies."

His eyes landed on a fat red cat who sat gazing up at him intently.

Oddly enough, he had the distinct impression that the cat had heard him.

And so he hurried off—time to get out of Dodge before all hell broke loose!

* * *

While Gran was discussing the state of affairs with Wilbur, the four of us exchanged views with Wilbur's cat, Kingman, our good friend.

"It's bad for business, that's for sure," said Kingman. "No customers means no money. And no money means no deliveries. And no deliveries means no customers, and no customers..." He smiled. "I'm repeating myself, aren't I?"

"That's all right, Kingman," said Brutus. "These are trying times. All of our humans are in a coma, and I do mean all of them."

"Except Gran," said Harriet.

We all glanced at the old lady, who now stood conferring with Wilbur and carrying out a whispered conversation. "She's a force of nature," said Kingman. "And so is Wilbur. Why do you think they've both been spared?"

"No idea," I confessed.

"Maybe because they're both old and not very nice?" Dooley suggested.

This elicited a smile on all of our faces. Dooley was right, of course. Neither Wilbur nor Gran are exactly known for their sunny personalities.

"But then how do you explain that?" said Harriet.

We looked where she was pointing, and much to our surprise we saw that Scarlett Canyon came hurrying up to us, accompanied by Clarice, another one of our good friends.

"Well, she's old," Kingman ventured. "Though it's true that she's a lot nicer than your Gran and my Wilbur."

He was right. Scarlett Canyon, Gran's best friend, is generally considered the nicest of the two friends. For one thing, she had recently agreed to adopt Clarice, formerly a feral street cat, who now lived a happy life in her new home.

"What's going on?" asked Clarice as she joined us. "People are dropping like flies. Is it something in the air? The food? The water? What?"

"No idea," I said. "Our own humans are all laid up at the hospital, except for Gran, who's the last one standing."

"And Grace," said Dooley. Gran had checked on Grace, and fortunately the kind lady who ran the daycare center hadn't been affected by the disease either.

"In my building at least half of the residents are sick," said Clarice. "It's a miracle Scarlett is still walking around. I can't imagine what would happen if she were to get sick, too."

I had to suppress a smile at this. Once upon a time, Clarice would have fought tooth and claw not to have to live in an apartment—or a prison cell, as she called it. She had certainly changed her tune.

"What's with this guy?" asked Kingman, gesturing to a funny-looking little man with a wisp of a mustache who was behaving very strangely indeed. Skittish, I would have said, as if he was suffering from a guilty conscience. When I gave him a curious stare, he practically jumped and then quickly hurried away.

"Who's he?" asked Harriet.

"Levi Kidner," said Kingman. "A regular customer. A lawyer, if I'm not mistaken."

Immediately, my interest was piqued. Acting on a hunch or gut feeling, if you will, I decided that maybe it behooved us to find out a little more about this funny little man. I may be revealing a flaw in my character, but as I see it, lawyers are, by and large, highly suspicious characters and are often up to no good. Contrary to actual crooks, though, they hardly ever serve time, possibly because they're too clever to stray too far from the straight and narrow, in spite of their transgressions.

"Max, where are you going?" Dooley asked.

"I'm going to follow this guy," I told him. "I'll be right back, don't worry."

For a moment, he wavered, then he came hurrying after me. "Can I tag along?"

I gave him a grateful smile. "I wouldn't have it any other way."

CHAPTER 13

*V*esta had apprised Wilbur of the events as they had unfolded in the last twenty-four hours when Scarlett came stepping into the store. She felt a powerful sense of relief to see her friend, looking as healthy and in fine fettle as always.

"You won't believe how happy I am to see you," she said as she even went so far as to give the other woman a hug—something that had never happened before. It just went to show how stricken she was by the fate that had befallen her family.

"Francis said he'd be here soon," said Wilbur as he checked his watch.

"Looks like the four of us are pretty much all that's left," said Scarlett.

"The last ones standing," Wilbur confirmed. "Which tells us what?"

"That we're made of sterner stuff," said Vesta, who couldn't explain it otherwise. She had told Wilbur about the tests that they had run on her at the hospital, and that they were going to give her the results when they had them.

"We need to do something," said Scarlett. "In my building alone more than half of the residents have been taken to the hospital. Even young people in their prime are falling like flies. And why? Nobody seems to know or they're not telling us."

On the news, Hampton Cove and the epidemic that held their small town in its grip was all they talked about. It was the number-one topic on all the big networks, and a hot topic in the news, trending on social media, and talked about across the country. Oddly enough, they were the only town to be hit by this mystery disease. Even neighboring towns like Happy Bays and Hampton Keys so far had been spared the same fate as its unfortunate neighbor. Which had led Vesta to conclude it must be something in their water supply.

"We need to get on this, and we need to get on this fast," she said. "Before the disease spreads to other towns, then the east coast, and soon the whole country."

"But where do we start?" asked Wilbur.

"The water supply," Vesta said. "It's the only thing that makes sense."

She had gone down the internet rabbit hole to try and ascertain where Hampton Cove got its water from, and as it turned out, most of it came from the local lake, which was then filtered and made safe for consumption.

"Something must have happened to cause the water to go bad."

Outside, their cats awaited further developments, and she figured it wouldn't be a bad idea to enlist them for their purposes. Though when she looked closer, she saw that Max and Dooley had already skedaddled, perhaps carrying out their own, parallel inquiry. Leave it to Max to dig up the cause of all this mess.

Francis Reilly now walked in, his cat Shanille in his wake, both looking harried and drawn, as was to be expected. "If this keeps up, we'll be drowning in funerals soon," he lamented.

"So?" said Wilbur. "Good for business, I'd say." They all gave the shopkeeper a withering look. "Too soon?" he said. "I thought so."

"Of my flock alone, about fifty to sixty percent is in the hospital right now," said Father Reilly. "And the rest don't look too good either. It's a miracle that we're still standing." He quickly made the sign of the cross to thank a merciful Lord for blessing him with such robust health. "So, what's the plan?"

Now that the four members of the neighborhood watch were gathered, it was time for action. And so she told Francis about her theory that something must have gone wrong at the water plant. "I suggest we head over there and find out what's going on. Either this was an accident, and someone pulled the wrong lever or pushed the wrong button, or…" She fixed them with a meaningful look.

"Or it was deliberate?" asked Francis, his eyes widening in shock.

Vesta nodded slowly. "A terrorist attack on our town. Which means that we should be prepared for any contingency." She held up her stun gun. "I'm ready. Are you?"

Wilbur retrieved the baseball bat he kept next to his cash register, Scarlett took out the pepper spray they had bought on Black Friday last year, and Francis? He showed them his weapon of choice, which turned out to be a very large and heavy crucifix. "One hit of this, and they'll think twice about attacking our water supply," he assured them.

"Are you sure this is a good idea?" asked Scarlett. "Maybe we should talk to the police about our suspicions?"

"The police are all in the hospital," Vesta said. "Or at least most of them. And what's left are probably too busy to patrol the streets for looters and other scum of the earth."

Now that a large part of the town's population was out of commission, that meant that Hampton Cove had turned into paradise for thieves and burglars who would descend on the town like flies on a pile of cow dung, ready to feast their eyes and fill their pockets with as much loot as they could carry. It also meant that they didn't have much time to inspect the water plant before they'd patrol those very same streets and give the remaining cops a hand.

"Let's roll!" she said as she made a circular movement with her index finger.

Too bad the only vehicle she had at her disposal was Marge's old red Peugeot. But then she got a bright idea. "Say, who's driving those heavy-duty police trucks now that the cops are all out of commission?"

Scarlett shook her head. "Vesta, no."

"I think it's a good idea," said Wilbur.

"The Lord giveth, and the Lord taketh away," said Francis piously.

Vesta had no idea what that meant, but it certainly sounded like a blessing to her. And since a little encouragement went a long way with her, she decided that their first port of call would be the police station to commandeer a vehicle.

CHAPTER 14

"Where is he going, do you think, Max?"

"I have no idea, Dooley," I said.

We had been following this strange little man for twenty minutes now and still hadn't arrived at our destination. Wherever he was heading, it certainly wasn't anywhere familiar. We had left downtown Hampton Cove behind and were now on the outskirts of our town. And as we walked along, suddenly a bird swooped low and deposited something on top of the lawyer's head. He cried out and shook his fist at the bird, who disappeared from view after having carried out its attack.

"What happened?" asked Dooley.

"I think that bird just pooped on the guy's head," I said.

"But why, Max? What's with all the pooping birds lately?"

The man neatly wiped his head with a handkerchief, which he seemed to carry on his person for just this type of contingency, then continued his long trek through town. Finally, he arrived at a nice home that didn't look all that different from our own home, opened the little gate, and passed through. Moments later, he opened the front door with a key and disappeared inside.

"So now what?" asked Dooley.

"Now we wait," I said.

And since we had developed an appetite after all of that walking and wanted to give our paws a respite and our stomachs a treat, we rounded the house and went in search of a bite to eat. A recent survey had revealed that sixty-six percent of American households own a pet, which means that we had a sixty-six percent chance of finding nourishment in this man's kitchen.

"Bingo," I said when my eagle eyes spotted the pet flap.

"Are you sure about this, Max?" asked Dooley. "Maybe he doesn't like visitors."

"Like it or not, he's going to get them," I said resolutely and set paw for the pet flap. Moments later, we were standing inside a neatly appointed kitchen. It didn't meet the Nancy Meyers kitchen test of excellence, but it would do very nicely for us. Especially since that same eagle eye had already located the pet food bowls. As of yet, I wasn't sure whether Mr. Lawyer Man owned a cat or a dog, but I'm not picky when I'm starving. And as we took a tentative nibble, I soon decided that the lawyer was a cat person, as opposed to a dog person. That view was confirmed when a smallish orange-hued specimen trotted up to us, looking a little irate to find two perfect strangers dipping into his or her food supply.

"What do you think you're doing?" the cat asked a little feebly.

"Hi," I said, plastering my most ingratiating smile onto my face. "My name is Max, and this is Dooley. We're detectives working a very important case."

"Life and death," Dooley supplied helpfully.

"And your human—at least I assume that he is your

human—has been most instrumental in getting us the clues we need to crack this case."

"What case? What clues?" asked the cat, giving us a nervous look.

"The case of the pooping birds," I said, blurting out the first thing that came to mind.

The cat's expression immediately morphed into one of understanding. "Oh, I see. I thought I smelled something funny. Has that bird been at it again?"

"He has," I said.

"What bird would that be?" asked Dooley.

"I don't know his name, but he seems to have it in for Levi. Keeps following him around and using his head as target practice."

"How many times has this happened?" I asked, intrigued in spite of myself.

"Oh, um, about half a dozen times maybe? Why, has it happened again?"

"Yes, it has," I confirmed. "Just now, in fact." I shook my head. "Poor Levi."

"Yeah, poor Levi," said the cat and gave us a smile. "My name is Blossom, and Levi is my human." She eyed us with interest. "I've never met a cat detective before. So what have you found out?"

"Not much," said Dooley. "Except that your human is a lawyer."

"That, he is," Blossom agreed. "And a very good lawyer, too."

"Is that a fact?" I said. Blossom had interrupted our meal, but I felt that my stomach had to take a backseat while we threshed this thing out more thoroughly. "There have been a lot of people falling sick lately," I said. "You wouldn't happen to know anything about that, would you?"

"Oh, that's terrible. No, I haven't heard anything about anyone getting sick."

"Our humans are all sick," said Dooley. "Except Gran, but she's very tough."

"I'm so sorry," said Blossom, and I could see she really felt for us. "Do you think there's a connection between your humans getting sick and this pooping bird?"

I shared a look with Dooley. "It is true that poop contains germs," Dooley pointed out. "So maybe this mystery disease is being spread by this bird?"

I tried to remember if the bird we'd seen carrying out the attack on Blossom's human was Clark. The problem is that all birds look the same to me—or mostly so. I know I probably shouldn't be admitting this, but it's true. When I saw that Blossom was staring at me, I explained, "We met a bird this morning named Clark, and he said that bad things were about to happen in Hampton Cove. Something to do with pesticides and the development of a field located directly behind our home. Though I really don't see the connection with your human, to be honest. Except that for some reason, a bird has it in for him."

"Blossom, let's go," suddenly a voice rang out, and Levi stepped into the kitchen. Great was his surprise when he found three cats where he had expected just the one. Then he narrowed his eyes at me. "Aren't you the cat I saw in town just now?"

"Guilty as charged," I said, and since I sensed that the animosity was strong in this one, I decided that a tactical retreat was in order. "Dooley, let's go," I said. And to Blossom, "See you later, Blossom. Nice to meet you."

And as we hurried out through the pet flap, Dooley added, "And thank you for the food!"

CHAPTER 15

Vesta was starting to get a little impatient when, after ten minutes, Max and Dooley still hadn't turned up. She wanted to get her mission started, and she wanted to start it right now, without delay. But she also didn't want to get going without Max, who was probably the smartest cat she knew, and whose input she greatly appreciated. And as they stood waiting for the large blorange cat to return from whatever mission he had embarked on, a man came walking into the store who looked vaguely familiar. He was one of the rare few who had escaped the dreadful disease that was tearing through her beloved town like a tornado. Though truth be told, he didn't look very healthy. Pale and drawn, she had the impression he wasn't long for this world.

"What can I do for you, Brenton?" asked Wilbur, ever the salesman, even in these unprecedented times.

"Just the usual, Wilbur," said the man in subdued tones. And when the shopkeeper unearthed a packet of cigarettes from behind the counter, he gave him a grateful albeit weak smile.

"Terrible business, isn't it?" said Wilbur, who had elevated small talk to an art form.

"Yeah, terrible, terrible," the man murmured as he paid for his wares.

"Say, you're not looking too hot yourself," said Wilbur. "Are you sure you're all right?"

"I just found out I've got an ulcer," said the man. He grimaced. "Stress-related, according to the specialist I saw."

"You work too hard," said Wilbur.

"I really do," the man agreed. He raised a hand. "Well, I'll be seeing you, Wilbur."

"Yeah, see you around, Brenton."

"Wait a minute," said Scarlett suddenly. "Brenton? Brenton Brooke?"

The man looked startled, as if he'd just been caught out in a lie. "Yes?" he said in feeble tones.

"Scarlett!" said Scarlett. "We went out once, remember?"

The man clearly couldn't remember at all, but he did his utmost to hide this fact by plastering a weak smile onto his face. "Of course—Scarlett…"

"Canyon. We never did get to go on that second date, did we?"

"No… no, we didn't."

"So what are you up to these days, Brenton? If I remember correctly, last time we met you said you were an architect?"

"I still am," said Brenton, his eyes flitting to the door as a way of escape from this awkward conversation with an old flame—who wasn't much of a flame if Vesta wasn't mistaken.

"So what are you building?" asked Scarlett.

"Oh, this and that," said the man vaguely. "And that and this, you know."

"That's interesting," said Scarlett, who had never met a

man she didn't like, even if he looked like a mussel. "We should get together some time. Catch up."

"I would like that," said Brenton, though clearly getting together with Scarlett was the last thing he wanted. He held up his hand and shuffled in the direction of the exit. "Well, see you," he said.

"See you, Brenton," said Scarlett warmly.

And then the man made the great leap through the door, hurrying off with an alacrity that belied his former insipidness.

"Who was that?" asked Francis.

"Oh, just a guy I once met," said Scarlett. "He ordered lobster and made a real mess of things. He even managed to transmit part of his lobster to my décolletage. At the time, I thought he did it on purpose as a seduction technique, but when he canceled our second date, I realized he had simply bungled things. The poor guy probably felt so embarrassed he couldn't face me a second time."

"Brenton is one of the premier architects in Hampton Cove," said Wilbur. "He's the guy responsible for the new Town Hall they're thinking about erecting."

"They're building a new Town Hall?" asked Francis. "I didn't know that."

"There are all kinds of problems with the old building," said Wilbur. "Ranging from the plumbing to the wiring to the general layout. The thing is a fire trap. So they're planning to tear it down and start from scratch. Bring it up to code."

"I guess those plans will have to be delayed now," said Francis.

"Yeah, I guess so," said Wilbur. "Maybe that's why Brenton looked so bad. He's probably out of a job right now, same as the rest of us." He directed a look at Vesta. "So are we just going to stand around here or what?"

"I'm waiting for Max and Dooley to return," said Vesta.

Outside, the rest of the troupe looked as impatient as she was feeling, and just when she felt they couldn't wait any longer, Max and Dooley finally came hurrying up. "Finally!" she said. "Where have you guys been?"

"Following a hunch," said Dooley, a little out of breath.

"A hunch that didn't really pan out," Max admitted.

"But we did get a nice bite to eat," Dooley added.

And since the gang was complete again, it was time to move out and get this show on the road. So they set out for the police station, where Vesta planned to commandeer a police vehicle and perhaps some of that nice hardware the police like to collect in their perpetual fight against the criminal element. Wilbur might have his baseball bat and Francis his crucifix, but she didn't think that would suffice when confronted with the kind of looters who would flock to their streets come nightfall. It's best to be armed to the teeth to combat such vermin.

CHAPTER 16

It was a motley crew who moved out in the direction of the police station: the remnants of our family, along with an assorted variety of cats. And it would have probably attracted a lot of attention if the streets hadn't been more or less deserted. Not a lot of people had been left standing in Hampton Cove, but oddly enough the pet population hadn't been affected, which made me wonder why this mystery disease only attacked humans, not animals. It definitely was something to file away for later reflection. Right now, we were too busy trying to keep up with the four humans who made up the neighborhood watch, for they were determined to set a scorching pace in their haste to resolve this case.

"So what did you find out, Max?" asked Harriet.

"Nothing much," I said. "Just a guy wanting to get out of town as soon as possible. A lawyer, you know."

"He had a cat named Blossom," Dooley supplied helpfully. "And she shared her food with us, which was nice."

"Oh, food," said Kingman with a sigh. "I wish I had some now."

We gave the voluminous cat an odd look. "But you just ate," Shanille pointed out. "You literally just ate. I saw you. We all did."

"Yeah, but I should have taken some for the road," Kingman explained. "What if I won't get anything more to eat for the rest of the day? I'll starve to death!"

"Don't worry about starving to death, Kingman," said Clarice. "I'll catch you a nice juicy rat along the way. A snack to tide you over, you know."

Kingman gave her a look of disgust but softened when he realized she was just trying to be nice. "Gee thanks, Clarice. That's very kind of you."

"Don't sweat it," said Clarice magnanimously. "There's rat for all of you."

I swallowed away a lump. The last thing I wanted was to find rat on the menu. And so I sincerely hoped this mission wouldn't take too long.

"We met an architect," said Brutus, apropos of nothing. "One of Scarlett's old flames. He's designing an entirely new Town Hall. He didn't look well, though."

And so the conversation flowed back and forth, at least until we had reached the police station, where we all ventured inside. Much to our relief, we found Dolores seated on her throne as usual, presiding over the police vestibule. "My God," she exclaimed the moment we walked up to her desk. "It's been quite the morning! Did you know that half the population of Hampton Cove has been taken ill? And the other half is worried out of their skulls and have been calling non-stop! So are you here to lend me a hand?"

"No, we're here to commandeer a vehicle," said Gran in no uncertain terms as she fixed the dispatcher-slash-desk-sergeant with a gimlet eye. "And don't give me that 'You're not a cop so you can't have one of our vehicles' look, Dolores. You know as well as I do that these are special circumstances, and special times call for special measures. So hand me those keys and hand me them something quick!"

The two ladies squared off for a moment, engaged in a battle of the wills, but then Dolores shrugged. "I guess we can use the extra hand, seeing as pretty much all of our officers are out of commission. Even the Chief is laid up sick."

"I know," said Gran.

"And his wife."

"I know."

"And Chase."

"I know! Now, are you going to give me those keys or what?"

And so Dolores dug into a lockbox and handed over a set of keys. "Take good care of her," she advised. "This vehicle belongs to the Chief himself."

"My son," Gran reminded her.

"So what are you up to?" asked Dolores.

"We're going to inspect the water plant," Scarlett revealed.

"Oh, so you think there's something in the water, huh?"

"That's exactly what we think," said Wilbur.

"Personally, I don't think it's the water," said Dolores.

"Oh?" said Gran. "So what do you think is causing all of this?"

"Birds," said Dolores. "They've been pooping on people, and as we all know, bird poop carries diseases, so my guess is that the birds are sick, and they're transferring that disease to the humans in this town. Avian flu, or whatever."

"It's a possibility," Gran admitted. "But then how do you explain that some people get it and others don't?"

"Beats me," said Dolores with a shrug. "I guess the CDC should probably come in and take a closer look at the situation before it spreads."

"And are they? Taking a closer look?" asked Father Reilly.

"Not to my knowledge," said Dolores. "But then the

people who should be arranging all of that are also out of commission."

"So why don't *you* call them?" Scarlett suggested.

"Me!" said Dolores, pressing a hand to her chest.

"Yes, you," said Gran. "Look, this is the time for all of us to step up to the plate, Dolores. We all should do what we can to look into this matter, and if you know who to call up there in Washington or wherever, I suggest you pick up that phone right now and call them."

Dolores thought about this for a moment, then must have figured that Gran was making a good point and said, "Okay, fine. I'll call them. But I'm giving them my bird poop theory. Though I might also mention your water plant theory," she amended when Gran gave her another steel-eyed look. Her telephone chimed again, and she sighed. "It's been one after another. Randal has been running around like a headless chicken all morning. Burglaries, vandalism, break-ins... Now that a lot of inhabitants are in the hospital, it's paradise for criminals out there."

Just then, Officer Randal Skip came skipping into the building. "False alarm," he told Dolores. He looked a little harried, I thought as he leaned against Dolores's desk. The dispatcher handed him a note that she ripped from her notepad.

"Got another one for you, Randal," she said as she picked up the phone.

Randal sighed as he studied the note. "All hell is breaking loose out there," he said. "I hadn't even had my breakfast yet when I was already called out for a burglary. Some lawyer whose offices had been ransacked. Neighbor called it in."

"We'll keep an eye out for you," Father Reilly promised as he placed a reassuring hand on the officer's back. Randal gave him a grateful look.

"At least the watch is still on the job," he said. "At least there's that."

CHAPTER 17

It wasn't long before we were trundling along on our way to the water processing plant. On the one hand, it was nice to be riding in a sturdy vehicle and not Gran's little old Peugeot, but on the other hand, it felt a little strange to be sitting in Uncle Alec's car while its owner was laid up at the hospital. A little sacrilegious, even. Though Gran didn't seem to be affected by such qualms.

"This is a pretty neat idea," she told her fellow watch members. "Once this is over, remind me to ask Alec to get us one exactly like this. The watch deserves it."

"We do deserve it," said Wilbur as he appreciatively glanced around the interior of the vehicle, which was of the more luxurious variety.

"Don't drive us into a pond this time, Vesta," Scarlett warned her friend.

"That was an accident," said Gran as she leaned over her steering wheel and peered out across the dashboard, pressing her foot down on the accelerator as far as it would go, all the while keeping the gear shift operating in the lower register, which caused the engine to whine in dismay.

"Pond?" asked Shanille.

"Last time we were out and about, Gran took a shortcut through the park," I explained. "And promptly drove her car into the duck pond."

Kingman shivered. "I shouldn't have come," he lamented. "This woman is going to get us all killed, the way she's driving!"

It was certainly true that Gran's driving style is an acquired taste, but since the four of us are used to it by now, we didn't even bat an eye when she zoomed right through a red light.

"It was red!" Father Reilly cried.

"Was it? I didn't notice," said Gran.

Some people really shouldn't be on the road!

But at least there was one advantage: we got to where we were going very fast indeed. Before long, she parked outside the water plant, and we all got out, some of us with shaky paws, others with an abject sense of relief.

"This is it, you guys," said Gran, pointing to the plant, located behind a perimeter fence. "This is where the rubber meets the road."

I had no idea what she meant by that, but when she dug into the boot of the car and took out a bolt cutter, I was starting to see that she had come fully prepared.

"Dark skies," Brutus muttered as he cast a nervous eye at the constellation of clouds that had gathered overhead.

He was right. The skies were indeed darkening very quickly, and as they did, I thought I could see lightning flashing in the distance, a sure sign that a storm was brewing. Overhead, dozens or perhaps even thousands of birds were circling, and judging from the shrieking sounds they produced, they weren't all that happy.

Suddenly, a flock of them swept down and seemed about to attack us!

"Hey!" said Scarlett as one of the birds came dangerously close to pecking her on the head. "Keep your distance, will you, bird?"

The bird had other designs for her, for on its next run, it actually delivered a message to Scarlett that fastened itself to her shoulder and made her howl in dismay.

"It pooped on me!" she cried. "That bird pooped on me!"

I tried to discern if the bird might be Clark, but by the time it had finished its thunder run, it had disappeared as fast as it had swept down.

"Is it Clark, you think, Max?" asked Dooley.

"I'm not sure," I said, peering at the skies. "It was too fast."

"They are really fast," Shanille said. "And angry!"

"Maybe Dolores is right," said Harrier. "Maybe it's bird flu." She darted a look at Scarlett. "And now Scarlett will get it next!"

Scarlett must have had the same thought, for she had retrieved a paper tissue and was frantically removing the detritus from her person. "I do NOT want to get sick!" she declared heatedly. "And certainly not because of some obnoxious bird!"

"It's not the birds," said Gran. "It's the water. There's something in the water."

We all gazed at the water plant, rising up ominously in the distance, and then as one person, we all set paw in that direction. Gran did the honors of cutting through the chain-link fence, and moments later, we were all crawling through.

"Isn't this criminal damage?" asked Wilbur nervously.

"If it is, it's for a good cause," said Father Reilly virtuously.

Oddly enough, the water plant appeared to be fully deserted, but then I guess these types of plants really run themselves, everything being handled by computers. But as we stood in front of the concrete block that housed the plant, it soon became clear that there were still people on site, as evidenced by a metal door opening nearby and a wizened old man appearing. He looked like a janitor.

"You're trespassing," he announced. "And trespassing something terrible."

"We're members of the neighborhood watch," Gran announced, producing her badge. On cue, the three other members also produced their badges, and the old man blinked.

"Oh," he said. "Well, I guess that's all right then. So what are you doing here?"

"We have reason to believe that the water plant is responsible for the epidemic that's hit Hampton Cove," said Gran. "And we're here to inspect it."

"Well, go right ahead," said the man as he opened the door a little wider. "Though I can assure you that everything's up to snuff."

"We'll see about that," said Gran, and we all ventured inside.

"Are you the janitor?" asked Scarlett, voicing a thought I think we all shared.

The man bridled a little. "I'm the chief engineer. Linwood Catling at your service."

"Well, Linwood," said Gran. "There's something wrong with your water, and we're here to find out what it is."

The man puffed out his chest. "I can assure you—"

"Yes, yes, yes," said Gran impatiently. "You can assure all you want, but I've got a town full of sick people out there, so something is very wrong."

"Not my problem," said the engineer with a shrug. "My job is to make sure the water is fine, and I can assure you—"

"The water is not fine," said Wilbur. "The water is poisoned."

"Impossible!" said the man. "Absolutely out of the question!"

Just then, behind us, all hell broke loose, as a thunderstorm to end all thunderstorms descended upon the world. Rain lashed the tarmac, and the engineer quickly closed the metal door and locked it. So we were now inside the concrete bunker that housed the water plant, and it was up to us to find out what was going on. To ensure the engineer offered all possible assistance, Gran fixed him with a stern-faced look. "It's time to confess, Linwood. You did this, didn't you?"

"What? No!" said the old man.

"Are you working with a foreign enemy? How much are they paying you? Is it the Russians? The Chinese? The Portuguese?"

"You must be crazy, lady!"

"Have you no shame?"

"Look, you're barking up the wrong tree, all right? There's nothing wrong with the water! Here, let me prove it to you." And he took out a water bottle from his pocket, unscrewed the cap, and put it to his lips before quaffing deeply. Having drained the bottle, he wiped his lips and said, "This is water from our plant. Now would I be drinking it if I thought it was dodgy? Of course not."

The members of the watch shared looks of uncertainty.

But Gran wasn't so easily fooled by this display.

"Show us the plant," she snapped.

The engineer sighed. "All right, fine."

And he led the way to the inner workings of the plant.

"Oh goodie, Max," said Dooley. "It's just like a Discovery Channel documentary—only real!"

"Oh goodie," I murmured. Frankly, I wasn't all that interested to see how a water plant worked, exactly. But once Gran gets something in her head...

CHAPTER 18

Gran had given us a surreptitious sign, indicating she wanted us to stray from the beaten path and give the place a closer scrutiny, out of sight of our official tour guide. And so while the four members of the watch followed the engineer, the seven of us ventured elsewhere.

"This place is so big," said Shanille. "Aren't you afraid we'll get lost, Max?"

"I'm sure we'll manage," I said, with more certainty than I was actually feeling.

Shanille was right that the water plant was pretty elaborate, and that if we weren't careful, we might never find the way out. But as I've been in the habit of trusting my instincts in the past, I was hoping they wouldn't let me down now.

Clarice stuck her nose in the air. "I smell... rats," she said with a look of delight. "And plenty of them!"

"Maybe it's the rats that did this," Kingman suggested. "Maybe a dead rat got into the water supply, and that's how the water got poisoned."

"A dead rat would only add some necessary protein," said Clarice. "And enhance the health and safety of Hampton

Cove's inhabitants. No, there must be some other explanation." But then her face cleared. "A dead bird could have dropped into one of the water tanks, and that's how the poison spread."

We had been navigating the corridors of the plant and all of a sudden found ourselves in a very large room with several water basins. And as we surveyed our new surroundings, I wondered if Clarice didn't have a point. I looked up at the ceiling, at least a hundred feet above us. I could see ventilation shafts up there, so was it so hard to imagine that a bird might have gotten in, or some other creature, and had dropped down into one of these massive tanks and died?

"I'll never drink water from the tap again," Harriet said. "Only bottled water for me, you guys. Imagine what bugs are in this water. Bugs and birds and rats!"

We were standing at the edge of one of the big basins, and as we gazed down, I imagined exactly what Harriet was suggesting and could see it vividly.

"Nonsense," said Shanille firmly. "All of this water is filtered, so if there is a dead bird in there, or a dead rat or whatever, it will be filtered out. Plus, there are countless safety measures and tests being done on a daily basis to make sure this water is safe for both human and feline consumption. No, if something ended up in the water it's because of some human error—or design."

Her words echoed Gran's accusations leveled at the engineer, and they sent shivers up and down all of our spines.

Suddenly, Clarice uttered a happy cry, and before we could stop her, she was up and away, flitting between the basins and disappearing from view.

"Where did she go off to?" asked Shanille.

"She must have seen a rat," said Kingman.

"Clarice, it's fine!" Dooley yelled. "We don't want a rat!"

But Clarice was gone and stayed gone. "Oh, dear," I said. "I hope she'll find her way back to us."

"I wouldn't worry about Clarice," said Kingman. "She can take care of herself."

Just then, the sound of voices approached, and more out of habit than anything else, we quickly hid behind a boxy metal construction that stood nearby.

"I thought that engineer said he was the only one here?" Shanille whispered.

"I guess he lied!" Kingman whispered back.

"I'm telling you, Titus," said one of the voices. "If this goes through, we'll have to completely redesign the system. And that will take years, not months."

"I'm sure they know what they're doing, Norris," said the second voice.

As I glanced from behind our makeshift hiding place, I saw that the voices belonged to two young men, both dressed in white coveralls. They looked like engineers, and no doubt worked at the plant.

"They'll have to double the capacity, easily," said Norris. "Which means a lot of double shifts in our near future, buddy boy."

"Yeah, I guess so," said Titus. "Which is a good thing for us, anyway."

"Unless the consortium takes over. They've got the right —and the know-how."

Kingman, whose stomach must have emptied already, emitted a tiny burp. It had both men look up. "Did you hear that?" asked Titus.

"It sounded like someone's stomach turning," said Norris.

"It came from over there," said his colleague, and pointed in our direction!

"I think we better skedaddle," said Brutus.

And so skedaddle, we did!

"It's cats!" said Titus. "How did they get in here?!"

"Filthy rats," Norris growled, clearly not a cat friend. "Catch them!"

And since being caught was the last thing we wanted, we hurried off as if our lives depended on it—which maybe they did! We ran as fast as our legs could carry us, but unfortunately we were at a disadvantage since we didn't know the way in that sprawling concrete dungeon. Moments later, we had zoomed down a long corridor, only to discover that it was a dead end! And so before long, we realized that we were trapped, with those cat catchers approaching fast!

"Now we've got you," said Titus, a nasty grin on his face.

"You're not getting away!" said Norris, equally unpleasant.

"Max, they're going to catch us!" said Dooley.

"We have to take a stand, you guys," said Brutus.

"Fight for our lives!" said Shanille.

"So what's the plan?" asked Harriet.

For some reason, they were all looking at me, but I could have told them that I was all out of ideas!

"We can try and run between their legs," Brutus suggested, taking charge. "They might catch some of us, but they won't catch all of us."

It didn't sound like a good plan to me, but at least it was something!

And so as we got ready to escape through these men's legs, suddenly a sort of low growling sound emanated from behind the two water engineers. It came from a portion of the corridor that was covered in darkness.

"What was that?" asked Titus.

"It sounded like a wild animal," said Norris.

They both looked a lot less sure of themselves already.

The sound intensified, both in volume and pitch, and

seemed to come from all over the place, due to the acoustics of the concrete bunker we were in.

"It's a wolf!" said Titus.

"It's a monster!" said Norris.

Suddenly the sound erupted in a screech so loud and terrifying it made my skin crawl. It certainly had a debilitating effect on the two men, who forgot all about catching us and broke into a run to safety instead, howling in fear.

When all was said and done, we found ourselves alone, facing this wolf or monster. We all huddled together, our eyes pinned to the darkness from where the horrible sounds had erupted when all of a sudden... Clarice walked up to us!

She had a big smile on her face. "Nice bit of pantomime, wouldn't you agree?"

We all laughed in abject relief. Clarice had saved us... again!

CHAPTER 19

*V*esta had her doubts about this engineer, who seemed determined to convince them that there was nothing wrong with the water they had all been drinking. Talk about the wool being pulled over their eyes!

She leaned into her friend Scarlett and whispered, "Watch this guy closely. And if he makes one wrong move, hit him with that pepper spray of yours—be ready!"

Scarlett nodded, giving her a look of appreciation for the way she had seen through this man's lies. Clearly he was the one behind this whole business with the epidemic raging through their town and had been tasked with the job of organizing the cover-up.

"Do you want me to sock him?" whispered Wilbur in her ear. "If I sock him now, nobody will be any the wiser."

"Not yet," she told her fellow watch member. "Wait until he makes a move, then hit him—and hit him hard. Don't miss—you might not get a second chance!"

"This water," said Father Reilly as he eyed the installations that the engineer was showing them with a nervous eye, "has it been blessed?"

The engineer frowned. "Why, no, of course not, Father. Why, do you think we should have it blessed?"

Father Reilly shrugged. "I don't see the harm. Maybe it will counterbalance the evil workings this water has wrought on my flock."

Linwood rolled his eyes and sighed. "As I've told you numerous times by now: there's absolutely nothing wrong with this water!"

"Yes, but—"

"But nothing! We adhere to the most stringent hygienic measures, and as such, we constantly verify every procedure designed to make sure we deliver a quality product."

"Where does the water come from?" asked Vesta as she eyed all the gauges and levers and other technical gizmos in the machine room where the engineer had taken them.

"Lake Mario," said the engineer.

The four exchanged looks of alarm. "But... that lake is full of all kinds of horrible things!" Wilbur exclaimed. "As a kid, I used to swim in there, and when I came home, my mother always made me take a shower because I smelled foul!"

"Kids pee in there," said Scarlett, wrinkling her nose. "Bugs pee in there. Fish pee in there. Everything pees in there. And then you make us drink that stuff?!"

"It's all cleaned!" the man exclaimed, clearly wondering why he'd been saddled with such a difficult audience. "We use all the different processes I've just explained to you to make sure the water is fit for consumption."

"So what about that pee?" asked Wilbur. "Is this like in the pool, where they add a dye to the water so you can see who's just peed in the pool?"

"No, it's not like in the pool," said the man, passing a weary hand across his brow. "No dyes are added to the water at all."

"But you admit you add all kinds of chemicals."

"Of course we add chemicals. It's a chemical process."

"I don't like it," said Scarlett. "As a kid I loved playing in my wading pool, but even after a couple of days, that pool was full of bugs. I can only imagine what the water from the lake must be like. And you make us drink that! Shame on you!"

"Oh, God," said the man and seemed to go a little weak at the knees all of a sudden. As he should, Vesta thought, for he'd foisted this epidemic on their town!

"Listen, I should probably arrest you on the spot," said Vesta. "But I'm going to give you one last chance to talk yourself out of this. Who ordered you to poison the good people of this town? Who!"

"Nobody ordered me to do anything!" said the guy.

Vesta gave him a look of satisfaction. "So you admit that you're responsible."

"Responsible for what?!"

"For poisoning us!" said Scarlett, and Vesta saw that she was gripping that pepper spray tightly, ready to attack.

She stayed her friend's hand, for they had arrived at a crucial moment. She could sense that the engineer was about to crack, and decided to deal the coup de grâce. "Admit to what you did, and I'll personally see to it that you get a reduced sentence. Judges love it when the bad guys show remorse, and hate it when they don't. This could take years off your sentence, Linwood. Think fast!"

"But I didn't do nothing!"

"Except put half the population of this town in the hospital," Wilbur pointed out.

"That's nothing to do with me," said the man. "If anything, our water should have helped them to combat the consequences of whatever disease they're afflicted with. Our water is clean and pure and good for your health. Can I help it that people prefer to drink soda or some other sugared drink?"

He held up a finger like a schoolteacher. "Drinking water straight from the tap is healthy, economical, and good for the environment. We should all be doing it."

"Not if it contains fish eggs," said Scarlett. "Or pond scum."

Just then, their cats came trotting into the room, causing the engineer to look up in alarm. "Where did they come from all of a sudden?"

"Those are my cats," said Vesta. Clearly, the engineer hadn't noticed them before. "They're my eyes and ears, and if you're hiding something—anything—they will have tracked it." She turned to her cats. "So what did you find?"

She didn't care that the engineer looked at her as if she was crazy. This was her do-or-die moment. The moment everything hinged on. All of Hampton Cove relied on her, and she was not going to let her people down!

"Nothing much," said Max. "Except that they really hate cats in here."

"We were almost caught," said Harriet. "But Clarice saved us."

"She really did," said Kingman warmly. "Saved our hides."

"Oh, just a small thing," said Clarice modestly.

"So has he confessed yet?" asked Brutus.

Vesta decided that it behooved her not to respond, but she couldn't deny that she was disappointed. She really thought that her cats would have unearthed the plant's dirty secret by now.

"They did mention something about a consortium that's going to require profound changes to the way the water plant operates," Max piped up.

Vesta pricked up her ears. Consortium? Profound changes?

"What can you tell me about the consortium?" she asked.

The engineer stared at her. "That's classified," he said.

"Classified my tush! Tell us, or else!"

Scarlett held up her pepper spray, Wilbur held up his baseball bat, Father Reilly had taken out his crucifix and was wielding it dangerously, and she was pointing her stun gun at the man, ready to fire at will.

The guy gulped once or twice, understanding he was outgunned, outnumbered, and outmaneuvered, and held up his hands. "Don't shoot!" he said in a small voice. "I'm just an engineer—doing what I've been told to do!"

"What did you do!" Vesta demanded. "And what's the consortium!"

"They're a group of investors," he said, his brow bedewed with sweat now. "I don't know much about them, except that they swept in here about a year ago, to organize a meeting with management, at which point we were told that the plant was being sold, but we didn't have to worry, as our job security was guaranteed."

"I think I've heard about these people," said Wilbur. "I think they're the same ones who want to build the new Town Hall."

"They've been buying up land all over town," said the engineer. "And houses."

"What do they want with all of that land and those houses?" asked Scarlett.

The engineer shrugged. "Beats me. I just work here, lady. I don't run the place."

And wasn't that just the truth. Vesta lowered her weapon, starting to see there were larger forces at work here. "This consortium, are they the ones who've been poisoning our water?" she demanded.

"Nobody is poisoning the water!" the guy cried.

Vesta studied the man's face for a moment, but finally had to admit that he seemed genuine enough. "Okay, so if it isn't the water, then what is causing this epidemic, huh? You're the clever one. So tell us what you think."

"Can I... Can I lower my arms now?"

She made a gesture of compliance, and the guy lowered his arms.

"Look, I'm not a doctor, all right? So I really can't tell you what's going on. But if I were you I'd take a closer look at—"

Just then, two more men strode in. And the moment Linwood saw them, he immediately clammed up.

"It's the cats!" said one of the guys. "Catch them!"

The next couple of minutes were a sort of free-for-all or pell-mell of sound and fury. The moment the first guy tried to grab Max, Vesta fired her stun gun at him, landing him on the floor, twitching and foaming at the mouth. When the second guy snatched up Clarice, the latter scratched him across the face, forcing him to let go and giving Scarlett the opportunity to release a steady stream of pepper spray in his direction, causing him to join his colleague on the floor.

When the dust settled, Linwood Catling was gone—having opted for the coward's way out by physically removing himself from the scene.

And since Vesta felt their business was concluded, the watch beat a hasty retreat. One thing was for sure: that old water engineer knew something, and she was determined to find out what it was.

CHAPTER 20

By the time we managed to find the exit to the water plant, Linwood was long gone. But that didn't deter Gran. She clearly felt that the engineer had more to say, and she wanted to find out what it was. And so she ushered us all into her squad car, engaged the flashy blue light and the police siren, and zoomed off in the direction of town.

"We'll catch up with him—just you wait and see," she said as she leaned over her steering wheel like a woman possessed—or a one-woman action figure.

Scarlett, Wilbur, and Father Reilly fidgeted nervously, and the seven of us weren't too well at ease either, but we knew better than to try and talk sense into the old lady.

"Who are we chasing?" asked Shanille, who had a hard time keeping up. "And why did they put those two men in the hospital just now?"

"We're chasing Linwood the water engineer," I explained.

"And I'm sure those two men will be fine," said Brutus. "Just a little dinged up and their pride may have taken a hit."

"They wanted to catch us and dump us into those big

basins," said Harriet. "And then they were going to dissolve us with the chemicals they use to get rid of the bugs and the fish and the ducks and the scum they suck up out of the lake."

Shanille gulped. "And to think Father Reilly always fills my bowl from the tap. Maybe I'll ask him to pour me water from the bottle from now on."

"I see him!" said Gran as she pointed to a car ahead of us.

"How do you know that's him?" asked Wilbur.

"Because he's driving a car from the water company."

She was right. The car on the road ahead of us was painted yellow and blue, the colors of the water company. It even sported the water company's logo, which was a big fish, which seemed a little ill-advised, speaking from a PR point of view.

"I'm going to ram him!" said Gran.

"Don't ram him!" Scarlett cried, while Father Reilly made the sign of the cross and checked if his seatbelt was securely fastened.

The car the man was driving was a smallish type and was no match for the powerful truck Gran was steering. The truck even had that steel bumper guard that gives oncoming traffic something to think about.

"I'm going in!" said Gran. "Wish me luck!"

But lucky for us, wiser councils prevailed. She had been honking her horn and flashing her lights while she drove right up to the other car's rear, almost nudging it with a loving—or not-so-loving—embrace. But now the other man relented and steered his vehicle off the road and pulled it to a stop. Gran parked right behind him and immediately exited the vehicle, looking like a woman on a mission.

"Why did you run!" she demanded as she walked right up to the guy.

"But I didn't," the elderly engineer said, looking a little white around the nostrils. It's an affliction often experienced by people coming face to face with Gran when she's in one of her moods. "My shift was over, so I decided to clock out."

"A likely story," said Gran, who clearly didn't believe a word the man said.

"You were trying to tell us something before," said Scarlett, deciding to be the good cop to Gran's bad one. "About the consortium? You said we had to talk to someone?"

The man looked up and down the road, as if anticipating more trouble, but when he was satisfied that no one was there, he lowered his voice and said, "You should talk to Ronnie Vincent."

"Who's he?" asked Gran.

"When management first informed us that the plant had been sold to this consortium, Ronnie was the one who handed out leaflets telling us to organize and unionize so we could stop the takeover. When that didn't happen, he told us that we should quit unless we wanted to be guilty of conspiring against the common good." He shrugged. "We all thought he was a kook, so we didn't pay him any attention. But now, with all these people getting sick…"

"Yes?" Scarlett urged.

"Well, I don't know. I can't help thinking that maybe he was on to something."

"Where can we find this Ronnie Vincent?" asked Gran.

The water engineer took a card out of his pocket and handed it over. "He gave me this. Though I have to warn you—he's a weird fish. A real conspiracy nut."

"It's not a conspiracy if it's actually happening," Wilbur pointed out.

Linwood nodded. "So maybe he was right all along—but even if he was, it's too late now."

"Why do you say that?" asked Gran.

"Well, because the plant was sold, wasn't it? Ownership was transferred last month. So officially, I work for the consortium now—and let me tell you, they don't like nosy parkers like you sticking their noses in. So if I were you, I'd be very careful."

"They actually told you not to talk to anyone?" asked Scarlett.

"We all had to sign a non-disclosure agreement when we went in to sign our new contracts." He grimaced. "The worst part was the ten-percent pay cut. That hurt. But it's not as if there are a lot of jobs for water engineers in Hampton Cove, and since most of us built a life down here, to uproot our families and move to the other side of the country didn't hold a lot of appeal, so we decided to take the pay cut and stay put. Though now I'm not so sure I did the right thing."

CHAPTER 21

As we watched the engineer drive off, and Gran was already coming up with suggestions for what we could do next, suddenly a large bird swooped down and deposited a large assortment of droppings on the collected company gathered below. This time I recognized the bird as Clark, and as Gran, Scarlett, Father Reilly, and Wilbur freely gave vent to their dismay by shaking their fists at the sky and yelling certain expressions that I won't repeat here, I tried to attract the bird's attention by distancing myself from the company and hollering his name.

"Clark, hey, Clark," I said, or words to that effect.

But unfortunately, either he didn't hear me or he chose to ignore me, possibly deriving a certain pleasure from bombarding people with the product of his bowel movement. I have known birds like him before, and where at first it starts out as a pleasant pastime, after a while it becomes a compulsion that is hard to shake.

Dooley joined me. "Was it Clark, you think, Max?"

"I'm sure it was," I said as I watched the raven fly off, no doubt to take in nourishment and gather strength so he could dive-bomb our humans again.

"But why does he keep doing this?"

"I have no idea."

"It's a warning," said Brutus, also walking up. "He wants to warn us about impending doom. Remember what he told us this morning?"

"About the pesticides?" I asked, for I remembered it well.

"That, and also the development. Clearly Clark knows things."

"He certainly does," I agreed.

Harriet came prancing up. "He missed!" she said. "I don't have a single thing on me!"

"He missed all of us," said Clarice, ambling over with Shanille and Kingman in tow. "He only hit the humans."

"He's getting better at this," said Kingman. "A real sharp-shooter."

"I just wish he would stop doing this," said Shanille fussily. "It's not proper, it's not nice, and most of all—he shouldn't do this to a man of God."

We glanced over at the humans and saw that Father Reilly had borne the brunt of the attack this time, especially the top of his head, which looked like an ice cream cone with extra topping. He was wiping it with a sad look on his face.

"When I get my paws on that bird," said Shanille in a menacing tone, for her human means a lot to her.

"I'm sure he has his reasons," I said.

But since Clark wasn't ready to give us a peek behind the curtain, so to speak, it was time to move on. So we all filed back into the car, and Gran took off.

"Where are we going?" asked Scarlett, who likes to stay on top of the itinerary, as any good traveler does.

"We're going to pay a visit to this Ronnie Vincent fellow," said a grim-faced Gran. "Hear what he has to say for himself."

She had tried his phone, but the number wasn't listed—but luckily he had scribbled his home address on the card.

"I'm not sure paying a visit to a self-proclaimed conspiracy nut is a good idea," said Father Reilly, who was still busy with a handkerchief to remove the last remnants of bird detritus from his person. "Maybe we should head back to the police station and report."

But Gran gave him a look of incredulity. "The police station? What do we need the police station for? The watch isn't accountable to them. We're a force unto ourselves, Francis, and don't you forget it."

"Oh, I know," said Father Reilly, "but perhaps new information has come to light that we should know about."

"There is no new information," said Gran, "except the information that we gather. Which is why we'll keep on gathering it until we have cracked this case."

It wasn't long before we had arrived at the home where Ronnie Vincent lived, and Gran parked across the street from the man's dwelling, which was a nice little bungalow that had been painted a bright orange with the roof a verdant green. It looked more like something a family of hobbits would live in. Which told us something about the character of Mr. Vincent.

"Okay, so this guy is obviously a little nutty, so if he becomes violent, I want you to have my back," said Gran, addressing her troops, which included her cats. "Make sure you're on high alert, is that understood?"

"Absolutely," said Scarlett, as she took a firmer grip on her can of pepper spray.

We got out of the car and crossed the street at a trot, for time was of the essence, and gathered on the front porch of the funny-looking bungalow. It didn't even have a normal bell but only a sturdy knocker in the shape of a swan's beak. After Gran had ascertained that everyone was ready for any contingency, she grabbed hold of the beak and let it drop on its designated metal plate, sending a message to anyone inside that visitors had arrived and desired urgent speech.

It wasn't long before the door was opened, and a woman appeared, looking a little suspicious when she found four senior citizens and seven cats on the mat.

"Yes?" she said.

"We're looking for Ronnie Vincent," said Gran. She briefly tapped her bony chest. "We're the neighborhood watch."

That didn't seem to hold any meaning to the woman, for her suspicion merely deepened. "What do you want with Ronnie?"

"We just want to talk to him," said Scarlett.

"About the consortium," Wilbur added.

"Rumor has it that he knows things," said Father Reilly.

The woman now took in the aged priest, and her expression softened. "Father Reilly, isn't it? I'm one of your parishioners at St. John's. You baptized our kids."

"Ah, of course," said the priest, nodding warmly as he clasped his hands together. "And how are the little ones?"

"Not so little anymore now, but they're fine—thanks for asking." She gave the man a smile. "I didn't know you were involved with the neighborhood watch."

"Since its inception," said Father Reilly. "I feel it's important to watch out for one another." He spread his arms. "Neighbor taking care of neighbor is the essence of humanity and a fine display of the Christian spirit, wouldn't you agree?"

"Oh, absolutely," said the woman. "Well, Ronnie isn't home right now. But if you want, I'll let him know that you dropped by."

"You wouldn't know anything about this consortium, would you?" asked Gran.

The woman shook her head. "I don't think Ronnie has mentioned it to me. Why? Is it important?"

"We think the consortium, whatever it is, is involved with this health crisis we're facing as a community," said Father Reilly. "Though right now the information is a little vague, which is why we were hoping your husband might be able to enlighten us."

The woman's face clouded. "I've been watching the news all morning. It's terrible, isn't it? They've closed the schools, so the kids are home right now. Thank God we're all safe and healthy—even my mom and dad and also Ronnie's family. So you think someone is actually responsible for this disease?"

"We think there's a good chance," Father Reilly confirmed.

"Well, I hope you find out who it is, and you can make them pay," said the woman. "Playing with people's lives like this shouldn't be allowed."

She then gave us Ronnie's current phone number—the one he reserved for family and friends only—and we said our goodbyes and went on our way.

"Nice lady," said Scarlett as we got back into the car.

"I've known her family for many years," said Father Reilly. "Her mom and dad come to church every Sunday. She and her husband not so much." He smiled. "I didn't know he was the Ronnie you mentioned. If I recall correctly, he's a fine upstanding citizen—not the crazy person the water engineer made him out to be."

"Well, we'll see about that soon enough," said Gran as she took out her phone and dialed Ronnie Vincent's number. Moments later the call connected, and the sound of a suspicious voice filled the car.

"Who is this?"

CHAPTER 22

Gran drew herself up a little. "My name is Vesta Muffin, and I'm the leader of the neighborhood watch. We've been following the events as they've unfolded with rising concern, and according to my information, you know more about the people responsible for the terrible epidemic that's been spreading like wildfire."

"Who told you?" asked the man curtly, not so easily lured into revealing all.

"Linwood Catling. He works as an engineer at the water plant. He told us you tried to warn them about a consortium taking over the plant earlier this year."

"That's correct," said the man. "And in the meantime, they have taken over."

"I know. We were at the plant just now," said Gran, giving her associates a nod, indicating she felt the conversation was heading in the right direction. "So what can you tell us about this consortium, Mr. Vincent? Do you think they're responsible for the disease that's plaguing Hampton Cove?"

"I'm sorry, but I'm not prepared to discuss this over the phone," said the man.

"Can we meet?" she asked. When he didn't respond, she added, "My daughter, her husband, my son and his wife, my granddaughter and her husband—they're all in the hospital right now, so if you have any information that can shed light on this dreadful business, I want to hear it."

After a long pause, he said, "All right. But no police."

"It'll just be me and the other members of the watch," she assured the man. And seven assorted cats—but he didn't need to know that.

When he gave her the address, we all looked up. It was Blake's field!

After Gran hung up, she tapped her phone against her chin. "This guy is extremely coy. When we meet, we'll have to make sure we don't spook him, or we'll never see or hear from him again. So let's do as he says and keep the cops out of this, all right?"

"Fine with me," said Scarlett.

"I don't know," said Father Reilly, looking concerned. "When a man says he doesn't want to involve the police, it automatically makes me suspicious about his motives. Why no police? And why all the secrecy?"

"Isn't it obvious?" asked Gran. "Because the people behind this whole business are extremely powerful—no doubt they're capable of making any investigation into their business affairs go away. They must have judges, cops, politicians on the payroll. Everything to make sure things go smoothly for them."

Her words were certainly cause for great concern, and for a moment no one spoke. Then all of a sudden, we heard the sound of a plane overhead, and a rain shower drenched the car, causing the windshield wipers to automatically activate and go into overdrive.

"What was that?!" Wilbur cried.

"Now I've had it," said Gran. "Overflying planes and

sudden rain showers—this can't be a coincidence." And so she pointed at the overflying plane, which was of the smallish crop duster variety. "Follow that plane!" And since she was the one behind the wheel of the car, she immediately started the engine, and moments later, she was indeed following that plane—which is easier said than done!

"You guys," said Brutus. "I think we better strap in. This is going to be a bumpy ride!"

And so we all dug our claws into the backseat, making sure we wouldn't be jostled about as Gran threw caution to the wind and drove like a maniac, all the while keeping her eye on that plane—and not so much on the road!

Lucky for us, there weren't a lot of cars on the road, owing to the fact that most of the drivers were probably laid up in the hospital being sick. So when Gran veered off the road a few times and ran a couple of red lights, she could do so with impunity—all in the interest of not losing sight of that plane!

"Be careful, Vesta," said Scarlett as she braced herself by putting a hand on the dashboard and her other hand gripping her chair firmly. "Watch out for that van!"

A van was indeed passing the intersection at a rapid speed, but instead of slowing down, Gran simply pushed down hard on the gas and managed to squeeze past the van, almost allowing it to clip our rear!

The van driver leaned on his horn, but Gran was a woman possessed and didn't even bat an eye.

"Why are you following that plane?" asked Father Reilly reasonably.

"Because it keeps spraying us with some noxious substance!" said Gran.

We all shared a look, for I hadn't yet put two and two together, but obviously Gran had. "What is she talking about?" asked Kingman.

"Well, every time this plane passes over, it starts raining," I explained. "But only locally. Like in very, very locally. As in just a few square feet are affected."

"Oh, so you think that it's the plane that drops the rain?" asked Dooley.

"Rain—or some other substance," I said, nodding.

"Now why didn't we think of that?" said Clarice, darting a look of admiration at Gran's back.

"Because Gran is in the zone," said Harriet. "The lady is on fire!"

That was certainly the case, and if she wasn't careful, soon we would all be on fire—literally! A large fuel truck approached from the other direction, and since Gran was driving on the wrong side of the road—possibly thinking she was British all of a sudden—it wouldn't be long before we were all toast!

"Watch out!" Scarlett screamed and gave the steering wheel a sudden yank.

Father Reilly, a little pale, suggested, "Maybe one of us should drive?" But Gran didn't even deign this with a response. She was in charge now—as well as charged up—and nothing and no one could stop her from catching that plane!

Soon, we passed a sign that said, 'You're leaving Hampton Cove. Visit again soon!' and wide-open fields stretched out on every side.

"At least here she won't be able to hit anything," Brutus murmured.

"I wouldn't be too sure about that," Harriet returned.

But luck was on our side, and no more incidents ensued. The plane, which had been flying lower and lower, now disappeared across the horizon, indicating that it had landed. "What's out there?" asked Scarlett.

"Reginald Keane Airfield," said Wilbur. "A small airstrip, mostly used by amateur pilots."

And as we rounded the next corner, from among the cornfields suddenly an air traffic control tower loomed up, and we saw that the plane we had been tracking was taxiing down the runway before pulling to a stop in front of a large hangar.

Gran parked her car by the side of the road as we studied the plane. For a moment, nothing happened, then the door opened, and a man crawled out.

"That's the guy we want," said Gran, pointing to the man. "Let's go!"

Her voice brooked no contest, and so before long we were hurrying along the road in the direction of the airfield, where an unsuspecting pilot was about to come face to face with a very irate old lady, eager to exchange a few words with him.

CHAPTER 23

When a person is suddenly confronted with a mob of people approaching him in a menacing fashion, the standard response is to flee—a prudent and wise decision. The pilot, when he saw Gran and her posse stomping up to him, clearly harboring ill will, chose to take the high road—or rather the only road—leading away from the airstrip. So he jumped into a neat little roadster and roared out of there, putting some safe distance between himself and the angry mini-mob at a speed of sixty miles per hour, leaving us all in the dust.

"Darn it!" said Gran, shaking her fist in frustration. "We almost had him!"

"And now we don't," said Kingman smartly, causing Gran to give him the evil eye.

"Now what?" asked Wilbur.

"Now we inspect that plane!" said Gran.

And so we all gathered around the small plane, which was indeed a crop duster, used by farmers to dust their crops with pesticides, insecticides, and every other 'cide' under the sun, hoping it would cause their crops to survive the onslaught of bugs, mites, or diseases, rendering their hard work tilling the soil null and void.

"Okay, so color me confused," said Father Reilly. "But what has this plane to do with anything?"

During our wild ride, Gran hadn't had time to dot any I's or cross any T's, but she did so now. "I've noticed that each time it rains, this plane happens to be flying overhead. So what if this sudden spate of diseases plaguing our town has nothing to do with the water supply but was caused by someone poisoning us from above?" She pointed to the smallish plane. "With this here plane?"

"Do you think it's the consortium that's behind this?" asked Scarlett.

"Wouldn't surprise me one bit," said Gran as she looked the plane over.

Unfortunately, none of us are experts in planes, so there wasn't a lot to be concluded from checking this particular specimen out. It looked like a regular plane, and if it had been up to any nefarious business, it was hard to determine.

"We need an expert," Gran finally concluded. "Someone who knows about planes." She darted a look at her posse. "Anyone know any experts?"

The three other watch members all shook their heads.

And as we stood around staring hard at the plane, suddenly a man came hurrying up. He was of the middle-aged variety, with a crop of white hair and a sort of craggy face. He was also ruggedly handsome, as the vernacular goes.

"Can I help you?"

"Vesta Muffin, neighborhood watch," said Gran, shaking the man's hand. "What can you tell us about this plane or its owner?"

The guy, who introduced himself as Kennith Rumsey, scratched his scalp. "The pilot is one Garry Wateridge, and the plane is registered to a company named Skillz. But I'm afraid that's all I can tell you."

"Do you own this airfield?" asked Scarlett, whose eyes were shiny, and whose lips had turned pouty. "It's a mighty fine little airfield. And so many fine planes."

Mr. Rumsey gave Scarlett an appreciative once-over, and his lips curled up into a smile. Like Scarlett, he seemed to like what he saw. "Yeah, this is my airfield. All mine, as far as the eye can see. Well, at least until the end of this runway."

"And this Garry Wateridge, he rents from you?" asked Gran.

"Yes, he does. He rents space in that hangar over there and also for the use of my infrastructure." He turned smiley eyes on Scarlett. "Why the interest?"

"Well, like I said, we're the neighborhood watch," said Gran. "And we have reason to believe that this plane has been involved in illegal activities."

The man blew out a breath of surprise. "Illegal activities, huh? And what kind of activities would that be?"

"Are you aware that there's a major epidemic raging through Hampton Cove?" asked Gran.

"A disease," said Scarlett. "Really terrible. Lots of people in the hospital."

"Yeah, of course I heard about that," said the man. "But what does that have to do with my airfield?"

"Maybe nothing—maybe everything," said Gran mysteriously.

"This plane may be carrying a dangerous substance," said Scarlett.

The man grinned. "Dangerous, huh?"

"Very dangerous," said Scarlett.

The man leaned against the plane. "Do you like danger, missy?"

"As a matter of fact, I do," said Scarlett, flashing her lashes at him.

Gran rolled her eyes. "Okay, can we stay with the program here? What load is this plane carrying, do you know?"

"Load?" asked the guy, flashing a lascivious grin at Scarlett.

"The cargo. The stuff it's been spraying. This is a crop duster, is it not?"

"It sure is," said the airfield owner. "Which means it sprays fertilizer. At least that's what I assume that stuff is. To be honest, I've never asked or checked."

"Can you check now?" asked Gran. "Please?"

The man reluctantly shifted his attention from Scarlett to Gran. "Why?"

"Just do it, will you? It's important."

For a moment I thought he'd refuse, telling Gran she needed to return with a warrant or something. But when Scarlett asked him where he kept his documents, and he said in his office, and she offered to escort him there, he was very eager to comply. And so we all set foot for the man's office, Scarlett talking a mile a minute about how she had always wanted to learn how to fly and if he could teach her.

"It'd be my honor," he said fervently, and it was obvious he meant it, too.

Before long, we had arrived at a low-slung building that housed the office and some other facilities, and as we entered, it soon became clear this was basically a small operation, with only a handful of people working there. And as Kennith led Scarlett into his office and firmly closed the door behind them, we were all relegated to the waiting area, where we had the company of a large potted fern.

And so the waiting game began. But since cats are not

very good at waiting around, we decided to go for a stroll. After all, you never know what you might find. And as we passed by Kennith's office and looked in through the window, we saw that he was on the phone, and Scarlett was on the floor—unconscious!

CHAPTER 24

We quickly rounded the corner and hurried inside again.

"Gran!" I cried. "It's Scarlett! That guy knocked her out!"

Or at least that's what I thought must have happened.

"When I get my claws on that man," Clarice growled as she strode up to the door and began meowing up a storm, scratching at the pane like a cat possessed.

Gran, who had been reading an aviation magazine, veered up from her seat and hurried to that very same door and started pounding it with her fist. "Hey, open up!" she yelled. "Open this door right now or I'm calling the cops!"

"I thought in this constellation *we* were the cops," said Wilbur, which wasn't helping much and earned him a scathing look from Gran.

"Knock down this door already, will you?" she said.

Wilbur gulped. "What, me? But how!"

"How should I know. Put your back into it. Or at least your shoulder."

"Francis, you do it," Wilbur suggested.

"Me!" said Father Reilly. He gingerly touched the limb under discussion. "I'm sorry, but I'm suffering from a touch of arthritis, and my doctor told me to take it easy. Knocking my shoulder against that door would definitely be a bad idea."

"And my shoulder isn't what it used to be either," Wilbur confessed.

"Oh, for crying out loud!" said Gran, and searched around for something she could use to break down that door. Finally, her eye landed on the small table that supported all of those aviation magazines, so she gestured for Father Reilly and Wilbur to help her pick it up. Together, the three of them held up the table, then aimed it at the door in a haphazard fashion, clearly not used to knocking down doors. As a consequence, the door didn't yield one inch. "Again!" said Gran.

And once more, they shoved the table against the pane. The end result was that the table fell apart in their hands, a part of it landing on Father Reilly's foot.

"Owowow!" the priest yowled as he danced on one foot while grabbing for the other one.

All of this noise must have attracted the attention of some of the other people working in the office, for two of them now came running.

"What's going on here?" asked the first one, a burly fellow with glasses as he studied the remnants of the little table, which had served its purpose—not.

"My friend is locked up in that office over there, and your boss has knocked her out cold," said Gran, pointing an accusing finger at the door. "Now what are you going to do about it?"

The man shared a look of astonishment with his colleague, then both of them shrugged, and the bespectacled one walked up to the door under discussion and gave it a deferential knock. "Boss? Is everything all right in there?" When no response came, he put his hand on the door handle and pushed open the door.

It wasn't even locked!

"Oh, dear," he said as he walked in.

And as we all stormed in after him, we saw that Scarlett was still on the floor, passed out, but of the airfield owner, there wasn't a single trace. The window was open, though, with a curtain gently billowing in the breeze.

"He escaped!" said Gran, hurrying over to the window and looking out.

As luck would have it, Kingman had decided to linger, and now announced, "He took off in an airplane." He pointed in the direction of said plane, and we saw that he was right. The problem was that the plane was already taxiing down the runway, and as we all watched on, it took off and disappeared into the horizon.

"Darn it," said Gran, voicing a sentiment we were all experiencing.

Father Reilly had knelt down next to Scarlett and was trying to bring her to—or read her last rites, I'm not sure which. At any rate, he wasn't having a lot of luck, for she remained as unconscious as before. Next to Scarlett, I now saw, a billy club lay, of the sturdy, unyielding variety. It was the criminal's weapon of choice.

"She has a nasty bump on the back of her head," the priest announced.

"But why would he knock her out?" asked Wilbur. "That makes no sense."

"He must be in cahoots with the consortium," said Gran. She now sat down next to her friend and gently stroked her head. "Better call an ambulance. Looks like they've managed to take out one of our own." She then shook her fist at the sky—or rather the ceiling. "They won't get away with this!"

"Who won't get away with what?" asked the bespectacled one.

Gran eyed him suspiciously. For all we knew, he was one of 'they,' whoever they were. "I don't know what's going on here," she told the guy, "but I'm going to get to the bottom of this, you hear? So you better tell us all you know—or else!"

The guy frowned. "I'm sure I don't know what you mean, lady."

"Your boss knocked out my friend—because she was on to something. So start talking—now! And that goes for you, too, buddy boy," she told the other guy, who was a man with a ponytail but no hair on top of his head—a strange combination.

"I don't know what you want us to tell you," said Ponytail. "It's not like Kennith to do something like this."

"He *has* been behaving strangely these last couple of days," said the other man, whose name turned out to be Raymundo. "Closing his door when he had to make a call, hanging around after hours and meeting clients. I even asked him about it, but he said it was none of my business. He was very unpleasant about it."

"It's true," said Ponytail. "It isn't like Kennith to keep secrets from us."

"What clients were these?" asked Gran.

"I never saw them," said Raymundo. "And when I asked, he wouldn't say."

"I thought he was selling the airfield," said Ponytail.

"You're sure?" asked Raymundo.

"Why else wouldn't he tell us? Clearly he was trying to get rid of this place, and he was selling us out to some big investor who was going to cut us from the payroll." He held up his hands. "At least that's my impression. I could be wrong."

"We can find out easily enough," said Raymundo as he walked around his boss's desk and took a seat in the man's swivel chair. He tapped a few keys and frowned. "Any idea what Kennith's password could be, Louie?"

"Um… try his daughter's name, maybe? Or his wife's?"

"I did, but nothing doing."

"Rebecca's birthday?"

"Bingo. I'm in." Moments later, he produced a whistling sound. "Listen to this, 'In pursuance of our recent conversation, I trust that you will supply the necessary provisions for our plane to be stored and refueled as agreed. As stipulated by our arrangement, you will be relieved of your duties and replaced by our agent. Please remember to honor the confidentiality clause in your contract or face a penalty. Yours truly, X.'" He looked up. "Looks like you were right, Louie. He sold the airfield, and he didn't even tell us. So much for 'We're one big happy family.'"

Louie sighed. "I hate it when I'm right. Looks like we're all out of a job."

On the floor, Scarlett finally stirred, but when she tried to sit up, she groaned and touched a hand to her head. "Ouch," she said. "What happened? Where is Kennith?"

"Kennith knocked you out cold and fled the scene," said Gran. "That's what happened."

"He did?" asked Scarlett, looking disappointed. "And we were getting along so well. He was going to tell me all about who that crop duster belonged to and its flight schedule, but before he had the chance, someone switched off the light."

"No one switched off the light," said Father Reilly, patting her hand. "He hit you over the head with that thing over there. And then he took off in his plane."

Scarlett studied the billy club. "Oh. Well, that wasn't very nice of him."

"Talk about an understatement," said Clarice, who was still fuming for what that man had done to her human. Unsheathing her claws, she added, "Wait till I get my claws on that Kennith. He'll regret he ever laid a finger on my Scarlett!"

And I could very well believe her.

CHAPTER 25

Gran printed off the email that might provide a clue as to the new owners of the airfield and their intentions, and then it was time to head home and get ready for our rendezvous with Ronnie Vincent, who would hopefully be able to tell us more about what was going on. The trip home was a lot less eventful, partly because Scarlett's head was still hurting, and partly because there was no one to chase.

I, for one, was glad, for I'm not really cut out to be an action hero. If they ever make a new Indiana Jones movie, or choose a new James Bond, Hollywood producers don't have to come knocking on my door! They can, however, address their inquiries to Vesta Muffin, who clearly has all the qualifications for the job.

"I could do this for a living," she now announced.

Wilbur and Father Reilly exchanged worried glances.

"I mean, I'm pretty good at this thing, aren't I?"

"At what thing, exactly?" asked Father Reilly carefully.

"The daredevil stuff, of course. Breaking down doors and

chasing people in cars. I'm like that action woman—what's her name… The Equalizer?"

Wilbur smiled. "You don't look like an Equalizer." When Gran gave him a dirty look, he quickly amended his statement. "I mean, the Equalizer can't hold a candle to you. Obviously."

"Obviously," said Father Reilly quietly as he checked to see if he still had all his limbs after our recent hair-raising adventures.

"If I'd been quicker off the mark, I could have raced that Kennith fellow down the runway and prevented him from taking off. Now that would have been something."

"It sure would have been something," Wilbur agreed. Though I had the impression he was glad that Kennith had taken off without the watch trying to prevent him from doing so. We might not have survived the ordeal!

"Gran is really on fire, isn't she, Max?" said Dooley.

"She sure is," I said.

"It's because her family is in trouble," said Harriet. "It woke up the dragon in her. Mark my words, before this is all over, she will rain down hellfire on the culprits."

That was exactly what I was afraid of! Then again, something clearly had to be done, and if it was true that a larger conspiracy was being perpetrated here, it was just as well that Gran was unleashing her inner demons on those responsible.

Before long, we had arrived home, and since we still had plenty of time to kill before our meeting with Ronnie Vincent, we decided to have a bite to eat and take a nap. Unfortunately, that wasn't to be. At least not the nap part. For when we emerged from the house after having enjoyed a hearty meal, we encountered Rufus, our neighbors' dog, wanting to have a word with us.

The four members of the neighborhood watch were in

the kitchen, enjoying their dinner, and as Rufus trudged up to us, he said, "Is it true that all of your humans are in the hospital?"

"Unfortunately, it's true," I confirmed.

"Except Gran," said Dooley. "And Scarlett," he quickly added when Clarice gave him a pointed look. "And Wilbur and Father Reilly," he amended when Kingman and Shanille did the same. "But apart from them, they're all laid up in the hospital. We'll pay them a visit soon, but first we have to meet a man about a conspiracy."

"How are your humans, Rufus?" I asked.

"Oh, they're fine. Over the moon, in fact. Turns out we won't be moving to the other side of the country after all."

"You were moving?" asked Brutus.

The big sheepdog nodded. "Ted's company was bought by another, bigger company and since that company is headquartered in Oregon, we all thought we'd have to move there. But now it turns out that Ted's new bosses have decided to move their corporate headquarters to Hampton Cove, so we can stay put."

"So why aren't you celebrating?" asked Harriet.

Rufus sighed. "Because they're building their corporate headquarters right here."

"Here? Where here?" I asked.

"*Here* here. Right here where we are standing right now."

"I don't understand," I confessed. "They can't build their headquarters here, since we live here."

"Not for much longer," said Rufus. "According to what they told Ted and all of his colleagues, this neighborhood will cease to exist. In fact all of Hampton Cove will cease to exist in its current form. This," he said, gesturing at our home with his tail, "is all going to be razed to the ground to make space for a brand-new industrial park. They're calling it Silicon

Valley East, and they're planning to turn this whole town into its beating heart."

We were all mum for a moment as we let this sink in, and then we all spoke simultaneously.

"But they can't do that."

"That's terrible!"

"Impossible!"

"Are you sure?"

"No one will allow that."

"Ted is crazy."

"There's no way this is true!"

"I'm afraid it's a done deal," said Rufus. "It also means that we'll have to move, since our house will be torn down. They are going to give us a nice new place to live, though, on the edge of town, so at least that's a good thing, right? I just hope we'll still be neighbors. Oh, and one other thing. We'll all live in apartments from now on, so that's the not-so-nice part of the deal. But the apartments are very spacious and very modern—with all the appropriate amenities, so there's that."

"But… but they can't just tear down this entire neighborhood," I said. "Haven't they heard of this thing called private property? Homeownership?"

"I guess they've found a solution to get around that," said Rufus with a shrug. "Or at least that's what they told Ted and his colleagues. Look, I've got to go—Ted is taking me to the dog park for what may very well be the last time." He gave us a weak smile. "I just thought I'd tell you guys—just in case we never see each other again." And with these words, he shuffled off, a dog at the end of his rope.

CHAPTER 26

The time had come for our meeting with Ronnie Vincent, and all of us were present. We had told Gran about Rufus's revelations, and to say she was expressing concern wasn't even half of it: the lady was furious!

"They're not going to make me sell my house, no matter what!" she said.

I could have told her that the house wasn't hers to sell anyway, but that seemed like the best way to pour oil on troubled waters, so I wisely kept my tongue.

Blake's field was still the scene of plenty of people milling about, measuring things and constructing things and generally keeping busy, so it didn't seem like a good place for a secret meeting, which is why I was surprised that Mr. Vincent would have picked that particular spot. When we arrived at the entrance to the field—located one street over—it took a while before I understood that the white van parked along the street and offering a perfect view of the field belonged to our mystery man.

When we came walking up, the van's door slid open, and

a man appeared who introduced himself as Ronnie Vincent and invited us to join him inside. I have to say it was a little crowded in there, with five people and seven cats, but as soon as we stepped in, it became obvious what was going on: the van was filled with surveillance equipment, and clearly Ronnie had been keeping tabs on the construction that was going on across the street from where he'd parked his van.

"Neat set-up," said Gran appreciatively. "Are you with the police, Mr. Vincent?"

"Or the FBI?" asked Wilbur. "Or some other agency?"

"None of the above," said Ronnie, who was a stern-faced individual wearing a bandana and a tiny orange goatee. He was a very intense person, and I got the impression he had never cracked a smile his entire life. "I'm just an individual who's very concerned about what's going on in my home town. Just like you, I imagine, Vesta Muffin. Scarlett Canyon. Wilbur Vickery. Francis Reilly. The four founding members of the one and only neighborhood watch. It's an honor."

Gran murmured her appreciation, and so did the others. It didn't happen every day that someone actually expressed their support for the activities of the watch. Mostly people railed against them and tried to get rid of them. And here sat a man who not only knew who these people were but knew all about their work.

"And your cats, of course," said Ronnie. "An integral part of your operation, if I'm not mistaken. Max, Dooley, Harriet, Brutus, Shanille, Kingman, and Clarice. Welcome to my operation."

We stared at the guy. "Max, he knows our names!" said Dooley.

"Yeah, he does," I said, much surprised and also impressed.

"He sure did his homework," said Kingman, nodding.

"Does this mean he's been spying on us?" asked Clarice suspiciously.

"It means he knows his stuff," said Brutus. "And that's a good thing."

"I'll say it's a good thing," said Shanille. "This man means business."

"He's probably a fan," said Harriet, preening a little. "Maybe I should sing him a song? Just as a thank you? How about a nice aria?"

We all hastened to dissuade her from this idea. Now was not the time to burst into song. Now was the time to get hip on what was going on.

Harriet, slightly annoyed, closed her mouth and proceeded to pout.

"Okay, so I suggest you tell us what the big idea is," said Gran.

The man nodded. "What do you know?"

And so Gran told him about the water plant, about Kenneth Rumsey and the airfield, the plane, the people getting sick, and about the plans to demolish all of Hampton Cove and turn it into a new Silicon Valley. Ronnie looked impressed.

"You have found out a great deal already."

"So this disease," said Wilbur. "Is it in the water? The air? What?"

"Both," said Ronnie. "Part of it is in the air, in the chemicals that the folks in this town have been sprayed with, but also in the water, since that's the easiest way to poison an entire population, since we all use the water from the tap, even if it's just to make a cup of coffee or to brush our teeth or boil our potatoes."

"But why are some of us getting sick and others don't show any of the symptoms?" asked Scarlett.

"Because we're all part of an experiment," said Ronnie. "The whole idea is to put part of the population out of commission for the time being, mainly to create a panic and to drive down property prices. You probably will have noticed that already property prices in Hampton Cove are at rock bottom, which means that land and houses can be snapped up at bargain prices, and that's what's happening. But they can't put the entire town in the hospital, as that would attract too much attention and lead to a full-scale investigation. No virus will take out an entire population, so that's what they're going for."

"Who's they?" asked Father Reilly.

Ronnie took a deep breath. "It's probably best if I show you. He fiddled with a few buttons on his console, and one of the screens in the wall of screens lit up. A logo appeared, and then a sales pitch that looked very smooth and very professional. It was the typical pitch of a large corporation trying to get investors interested in its proposal. Only this one was more ambitious than most.

"This is the consortium," said Ronnie. "They were formed five years ago by a group of investors, most of them based here on Long Island. They've looked very closely at the success story that Silicon Valley has written and want to do the same over here. Only problem is space. Where do you build an industrial park as large as that in an area that's fully built up? The only way is to drastically rezone a large swath of Long Island and get rid of everything, then rebuild from scratch. Only problem is that no one will give permission for such a radical plan—especially the people who live in that area. And that's why they decided to go for the stealth approach. They carefully selected a location, then secretly started buying up land and houses while also putting the necessary people in place so they could get the permissions. Then when they had gone to the limit, they started the second phase of their plan: scare people away by creating a mass panic, driving down prices."

"But not everyone will be prepared to sell their home," said Scarlett. "Will they?"

"That's where part three of their plan comes into play," said Ronnie. "They now have the full support of the governor and also the local mayor to rezone the entire town of Hampton Cove and turn it from a residential area into a semi-industrial one. That way the people who refuse to sell will simply be expropriated."

"Charlene will never allow it," said Gran. "Never, never, never."

"That's why they had to put her in the hospital," said Ronnie. "Along with most of the council members. To be replaced with a new, more amenable team."

"But... can they do that?" asked Wilbur.

"They already did," said Ronnie. "As of this morning, Charlene Butterwick has been replaced as mayor by an interim mayor. Weston Pilbrow has taken over, and since he's paid by the consortium, he'll quickly push through the necessary changes so that the third part of the plan can be put into effect—effective immediately. I think you'll find that all of your homes are located on land that has been rezoned and, as such, are ripe for demolition." He arched a meaningful eyebrow. "Which means the bulldozers will be coming for you any moment now." He spread his arms. "This entire neighborhood will become the epicenter of a new economic heartland, with Blake's field as its base. Right here, where we are sitting, a completely new town will be created from scratch, with office towers, corporate headquarters, recreational zones, and at the perimeter new residential areas where the people who will populate these new office buildings will live."

"And Hampton Cove?" asked Gran with a noticeable quiver in her voice.

"Will cease to exist," said Ronnie. "In its place, new business communities will emerge and spread like an ink stain all over Long Island, until finally the entire island will be one big high-tech center. In other words: Silicon Valley East."

CHAPTER 27

"Okay, so what do you want us to do, Ronnie?" asked Gran.

"Yes, the watch is at your service," said Scarlett fervently.

"Absolutely," said Father Reilly. "One hundred percent."

"We can't let this happen," grunted Wilbur. "No way!"

Ronnie didn't smile, but there was a flicker in his eyes that indicated his approval of the enthusiasm our humans displayed. One could almost say he was touched. "Right now there's only one thing you can do," he said. "And that's do what you do best: patrol the streets of Hampton Cove and make sure that everyone is safe. With so many people in the hospital, there's always a chance that nefarious elements will take advantage by breaking into people's houses and stealing everything they can lay their hands on."

"That's what I said," said Gran excitedly. "Isn't that what I said?"

"That's exactly what you said," Scarlett agreed wholeheartedly.

"But don't you want us to alert the authorities?" asked Wilbur.

"Yes, we have to stop these people from destroying our town," said Father Reilly. "Go all the way to Washington if we have to—right up to the President!"

"I'm afraid we don't know how high up this conspiracy runs," said Ronnie. "A project like this must be years in the making, with lots of moving parts and lots of people involved. I'm only now beginning to uncover the breadth of the deception, and I've been at this for months now—ever since I first learned of it."

"How did you find out?" asked Gran.

"Yes, what is it that you do, exactly?" asked Scarlett.

Wilbur pointed at the man. "Don't tell me—reporter?"

Ronnie gave a deferential nod. "You got me. I'm a journalist. Only when I started to dig a little deeper into this business and suggested to my editor we run the story, he promptly fired me. Turns out the same investors who are behind this Silicon Valley East business also own the paper I used to work for."

"Tough luck," said Gran commiseratively.

"And so I decided to do it alone. Uncover as much as I could find out, and then expose these people to the world once I knew all the sordid details." He shook his head. "It's been a tough slog, but I feel I'm finally getting somewhere."

"And now you've got us," said Wilbur, placing a well-meaning hand on the brave journalist's shoulder.

"Yeah, you no longer have to do this all by yourself," Father Reilly added in fatherly tones. "The watch has your back, young man, so fear not."

Ronnie didn't look like the kind of person who feared anything, but he still gave us a grateful look. "Let's keep each other informed. I've got an important meeting with an informant tonight, and hopefully he'll give me what I need: the final piece of the puzzle."

"And what's that?" asked Gran.

"The name of the man behind the curtain. The consortium's number one."

"Is that what you're calling him?" asked Scarlett, much interested.

"That's right. And once I know who he is, I'm going to expose him."

"What a brave man, Max," said Dooley.

"Extremely brave," I agreed.

"To go against these people takes a lot of courage," Brutus said. "Don't you agree, sugar biscuit?"

But Harriet's mind was busy with other ideas. "Once this new Silicon Valley has been built," she said, "they're going to need a mascot, right? Something to make them stand out? So maybe I should put my name forward?" When we all stared at her, she innocently asked, "What?"

"Harriet, but you can't sell out to the enemy!" said Shanille.

"What enemy? These people are building a very nice new town for us, where we will all live happily ever after. I'm sure it's going to be like paradise. And with me as their mascot, it will be pure heaven." She sighed happily. "I could even create a hymn or an anthem. How about it, Shanille?"

"How about what?!"

"Let's create a special song. Already I can feel the inspiration welling up inside me." And as she started to swell up like a balloon, preparatory to bursting into song, Brutus did the unthinkable and placed a paw on her mouth.

For a moment, no one spoke, too shocked to react, but then Brutus understood that he had made a faux-pas of monumental proportions, and quickly removed his paw. "It was a reflex reaction," he explained feebly.

"Brutus!" Harriet exploded. "How dare you lay a paw on my person and stop me from expressing my true self in song!"

"I'm sorry, precious angel," said Brutus weakly.

"Never, ever do that again, you hear!"

"I won't, chocolate drop," he assured her.

But at least he had stopped Harriet from singing, which would have been a disaster, since we were in such a confined space, and it could have been detrimental to our eardrums if she had given vent to her 'artistic self.'

The meeting had come to an end, and Ronnie swore us all to secrecy, which of course we did. That brave man was going to unmask the leader of the conspiracy, and if we could be instrumental in helping him, we were determined to do just that.

We all crawled out of the van, glanced left and right to make sure we hadn't been seen, and then hurried off in the direction of home. Gran had planned to pay a visit to the hospital to see our family and find out how they were doing, and then we'd all go out on patrol to make sure that the streets of Hampton Cove were as free of the criminal element as possible.

In other words, we had an important job to do!

CHAPTER 28

We found our family members in much the same state we had left them: unresponsive and being taken care of by the hospital staff, who had their hands full with the steady influx of new patients. Since there were so many of them at this point, they had to find extra beds to accommodate everyone.

"When they wake up, they'll be so happy to see each other," said Dooley.

"*If* they ever wake up," said Clarice, voicing the critical note.

"They *have* to wake up," said Shanille. "I've been praying for them non-stop, and I'm sure so has Father Reilly." She raised her eyes heavenward as she folded her paws in prayer once more. "In fact, I'll do it again right now. Tell me if it works."

She closed her eyes, and as we watched her lips move, I darted a keen look at Odelia, next to whose bed Gran had placed us, and hoped Shanille's prayers would work their magic. As far as I could tell, not much was happening, though.

Next to Odelia, Chase lay. Then there was Uncle Alec, Charlene, Marge, Tex.

Gran was holding her son's hand, intently gazing at the man and hoping he would wake up, but so far the big guy wasn't stirring, and neither were the others.

"We should have asked Ronnie if there wasn't some kind of countermeasure against this poison," said Scarlett now.

"Yeah, something to flush this wicked stuff out of their system," said Wilbur.

"If Ronnie knew what to give them, he would have told us," said Father Reilly. He, too, had folded his hands in prayer and was trying to work a miracle.

A nurse drifted into the room, took a good look at the clowder of cats sitting at Odelia's bed, shook her head, and disappeared again. Under normal circumstances, cats aren't allowed in the hospital, but these were desperate times, and Gran had explained how we were all pining for our humans.

Harriet wandered over to Charlene, who looked like an angel in her hospital bed.

"I just wish there was something more we could do," said our friend. "Maybe if I sing a song?"

"Noooo!" we all cried simultaneously.

"But it's common knowledge that music has a profound effect on comatose patients," Harriet argued. "And I can let them hear the hymn I've been working on."

"What hymn?" asked Kingman, curious in spite of himself.

"Oh, just a little thing I've been playing with," said Harriet modestly. "In case these consortium people ask me to become their mascot."

"You can't be a mascot for the consortium, Harriet," said Clarice. "That would be hobnobbing with the enemy and would make you as bad as they are."

"But it's not all bad," said Harriet. "If they're going to

build us nice new homes and give this whole region a new lease on life, it might be the best thing that could have happened to us."

"Tell that to them!" said Clarice, pointing to our comatose families.

Harriet wavered. "Yes, I guess that wasn't a very kind thing to do."

"Kind!" cried Clarice. "Kind!!! That was a dirty rotten trick to play!"

"Okay, just a few notes," said Harriet, and before we could stop her, launched into a song that sounded suspiciously a lot like Celine Dion's *"My Heart Will Go On."*

"Near, far, wherever you are!" she belted.

Her voice cut through us all like nails on a chalkboard, and as we tried to put our paws to our ears to mitigate the agony, all of a sudden Odelia stirred. First she frowned, and then she smacked her lips, as if trying to say something.

"It's working!" said Brutus. "Keep going, sweet cheeks—keep going!"

"Once more, you open the door!" Harriet screeched like a cat possessed.

A pained look came over Odelia's face, as if something was annoying her, which I could sympathize with, for Harriet's voice was annoying me something terrific! And then suddenly the unimaginable happened: Odelia's eyes suddenly flashed open and she stared at the ceiling for a moment, before yelling, "Stop!"

Promptly Harriet stopped singing her 'hymn,' and we all looked on with bated breath. In the other beds, the other patients also stirred, opening their eyes and becoming restless. Machines started beeping all over the room, and suddenly a flock of nurses hurried in, ushered us all out of the room, and started attending to their patients, who were all suffering from some strange malady.

I could have told them what malady this was, but no one ever listens to a cat.

And as we waited in the corridor, Harriet said triumphantly, "I told you!"

"Yes, you did," said Brutus proudly. "I think you cured them with the beauty of your voice, snow pea. With the sheer loveliness of your inspired song!"

"Maybe I'll do it again," said Harriet. "Only this time for the whole hospital!"

"Noooo!" we all yelled, causing her to frown in dismay.

As it turned out, the patients had indeed all suffered some mysterious episode, and by the time we were all allowed back in the room, they were all awake but looking extremely groggy and confused.

"Where are we?" asked Odelia. "What happened?"

"I remember we came to visit your mother," said Chase. "And then… nothing."

And so it was up to Gran to fill them in on some of the events as they had transpired these last couple of hours. She decided not to tell them about the big conspiracy, as they weren't in a fit state to absorb all of that information, but at least they were on the mend—and truth be told, Harriet's singing seemed to have been instrumental in that. Or had it?

"It was my prayer," said Shanille. "It finally worked."

"No, it was my singing!" said Harriet. "It touched their hearts!"

"More like shredded their eardrums," said Clarice.

Harriet cut her a dirty look but refrained from comment.

"It was my thoughts," said Gran. "I sent healing thoughts all the time."

"So did I," said Scarlett. "I visualized they would wake up, and they did!"

"I knew they'd snap out of it," said Wilbur. "And my hunches are never wrong."

"Hallelujah!" Father Reilly caroled. "It was my prayers! They were answered!"

Like they say: success has many fathers.

CHAPTER 29

Odelia and the rest of her family were still too weak to leave the hospital, but at least we knew they'd be all right, which was definitely a load off our minds! Before long, we had arrived home, where Gran fed us and also herself and her fellow members of the watch, and then it was time to do as Ronnie had instructed and go on patrol. And so once again we all filed into that car, Gran assumed her position behind the wheel, and we settled in for a long night of vigilance.

As luck would have it, the streets were quiet during the first part of the night, and as Gran slowly navigated the deserted ways and byways of our neighborhood and beyond, not a creature stirred, and not a criminal either, which was a good thing.

"Looks like the criminals are also laid up in the hospital," said Wilbur.

"Yes, that poison the consortium spread had an ill effect on everyone," said Gran. "Indiscriminate of age, gender, race, or how clear your conscience is."

"In other words, a very democratic poison," said Scarlett, nodding.

"I think we should pray some more," said Father Reilly. "So that all of our dear friends and loved ones will wake up and be able to shake off the deleterious effect of whatever drug they've been fed. So let's all fold our hands in prayer."

"Not you, Gran!" I said warningly when Gran took her hands off the wheel.

And as Scarlett, Wilbur, Father Reilly, and the rest of us all made to close our eyes to pray, I suddenly thought I saw something. A flicker of light that seemed to come from somewhere up ahead. Though when I looked a little closer, I saw that it was a reflection in the rearview mirror.

"Gran, what's that behind us?" I asked.

Gran checked the mirror and frowned. "Looks like a car, and it's heading our way—fast!" Immediately, she increased the speed of our own vehicle, and moments later, while most of the passengers were still murmuring their prayers, we were being pursued by this mystery vehicle that had turned up out of nowhere!

"Can you stop shaking the car, Vesta?" asked Scarlett. "I'm trying to pray here, you know."

"Pray for us," Gran advised. "We're being chased by some unknown pursuer!"

The others all opened their eyes and as they craned their heads to look behind us, suddenly the car that was chasing us came roaring up from behind and hit us in the rear fender!

"Hey, what does he think he's doing!" Wilbur demanded, shaking his fist.

Once more, the car came racing up and hit us again.

"Good thing I'm such an excellent driver," said Gran as she gripped the steering wheel very tightly indeed.

But when the car hit us a third time, she couldn't keep the vehicle under control any longer, and as she steered us straight into a hedge, all the passengers screamed—yours truly included!

We slammed straight through that hedge, and our momentum then carried us right up to the house beyond, and it was with a loud crash that we landed against the side of the house, brickwork raining down all around us, and when the dust settled, we saw we were inside the kitchen of the place, with an old couple seated at the kitchen table, staring at us as if we were a group of aliens who had landed.

Behind us, suddenly the sound of a gun being fired rang out, and moments later whoever had been chasing us started using the car as a shooting target! We all ducked down, and so did the old couple, and as glass shattered overhead, for a moment we all feared for our lives. But then silence returned, and we heard a door slam, then an engine gun, and a car drove off with screeching tires.

"Looks like they're driving away," said Wilbur as he dusted some shards of glass from his person. He glanced in the back. "Kingman! Are you hurt?"

"Just a scratch," said Kingman.

"We're all fine!" said Harriet after she had checked her person for puncture marks.

"The car!" said Gran. "It's on fire!"

Unfortunately for us, the doors were all jammed, and as flames licked at the interior, it looked as if our final hour had struck!

"What y'all doing in there?" asked the old man now, who had walked up to us to take a closer look. His wife had more sense than to stand around asking questions. She now came hurrying up with a bucket in her hand, and then splashed it over us, through the broken windshield, treating us to a cold shower.

At least it put out the flames, which was a good thing. But then something seemed to spark in the engine, which was very much busted up, and the fire commenced afresh. Two more buckets did the trick, though, and as the couple helped us out of the car through the broken windshield, we were so grateful to be alive that we didn't even care that we were all soaking wet. Better wet than dead!

"They almost killed us," said Gran, after she had expressed her eternal gratitude to the old couple for saving our lives, and offering her apologies for wrecking their kitchen and partly demolishing their home.

"Who were they, you think?" asked Scarlett as she patted her hair, which looked a righteous mess.

"Must be goons sent by the consortium," said Wilbur. "Trying to take us out!"

"I hope and pray that Ronnie is all right," said Father Reilly. "If they tried to murder us, maybe they tried to do the same with him."

Gran quickly took out her phone, but as she tried to reach Ronnie, her face clouded. "I can't reach him," she said. "Either he's not picking up or…"

"Don't say it!" said Scarlett.

"…or he's dead."

CHAPTER 30

It was late by the time the police had finished carrying out their inquiries into the circumstances of our crash, and since we were all pretty knackered, we decided to enjoy a good night's sleep—for the part of the night that remained. We arrived home just in time to discover that someone had slipped a message through our mail slot, but since it's a little hard for cats to open envelopes, and Gran had turned in for the night, for a moment we were at a loss for how to proceed. Something told me that the message was an important one, especially since someone had scribbled 'IMPORTANT!' across the front of the envelope.

Harriet and Brutus had joined Gran next door, so it was up to Dooley and myself to make an executive decision.

"Let's rip it open," Dooley suggested. "It could be important."

"It *is* important," I pointed out. "It says so right there."

"So let's rip open the envelope and see what's inside."

And so it was decided. Dooley would hold on to the thing while I did my utmost to slice and dice until it gave up its contents. The end result was that the corridor was filled with paper cuttings, but at least we had the opportunity to take a closer look at this urgent missive sent from an unknown sender.

'Don't try to find me,' the message read. 'The consortium has won. RV.'

"RV?" asked Dooley. "Who's RV?"

"Ronnie Vincent, probably," I surmised.

"What does he mean by 'The consortium has won?'"

"They probably got to him," I said. "The same way they tried to get to us."

"This is getting awfully dangerous, don't you think, Max? Attacks on our person and car chases and people disappearing? This consortium is tough."

I smiled. "Pretty tough. But then I guess they've got a lot riding on this."

"So what do you suggest we do?"

"We show this message to Gran tomorrow, and let her decide. She is the leader of the watch, after all, so let's hope she has some bright idea of how to proceed."

Dooley didn't look entirely convinced, and frankly speaking I wasn't either. Gran may be a woman with nerves of steel, who doesn't back down, even in the face of danger or threats being made against her life, but she's not exactly a genius when it comes to coming up with a plan to thwart these types of conspiracies.

But since I didn't see what we could possibly do to put a stop to the dastardly plans of this consortium, I hoped that a good long nap would bring much-needed inspiration. And so Dooley and I settled on the couch, and before long were fast asleep. At least until we weren't, if you see what I mean.

A scratchy sound woke me up, and for a moment I wondered if I was dreaming, but as my ears pricked up of their own accord, I soon decided that someone was trying to break into our home!

"Dooley," I said, giving my friend a nudge. "Wake up!"

"The sky is falling!" he murmured, then opened his eyes. "What?"

"I think someone is trying to break in," I whispered.

For a moment we both listened as the scratchy sounds continued unabated, and finally, he decided that I was right. "Probably those consortium goons again!" Dooley said. "What do you think they want?"

"No idea. Evidence that we're on to them maybe?"

"But we're not on to them! We don't even know who they are!"

That wasn't entirely true. We knew at least a few people on their payroll, like Kennith, the airfield owner, the pilot flying that crop duster, and our water engineer Linwood—though the jury was still out on him. Possibly he was innocent and had simply felt things were getting a little dangerous for his liking.

Something clicked, and Dooley and I both hunkered down as our eyes stared into the darkness, ready for any contingency. And as the person entered the kitchen through the kitchen door, whose lock he had successfully jimmied, we were ready to either hide under the couch, or fight this denizen of the underworld with tooth and claw—literally.

For a moment, it was hard to make out the intruder's features, as he was operating fully in the dark. After a moment, I discerned that he was wearing a mask—never a good sign—and gloves—definitely a bad sign. And as he started rummaging around, possibly in search of any material related to the consortium that Odelia might have collected before she had succumbed to the mystery disease, I contemplated our possible solutions.

"We should attack!" said Dooley.

"Or hide under the couch!" I said.

It was a tough decision to make. In the end, the intruder

decided for us when he flicked on a flashlight and shone it straight at us. I don't know who was startled the most by this development. We all screamed, and then the intruder decided that discretion is the best part of valor and promptly skedaddled. As the nocturnal marauder ran out of the house, I caught a whiff of a strong body odor that contained notes of musk and something lemony. Our nemesis might be a bad egg, but at least he put a premium on personal hygiene, always a plus in my book.

"He's gone, Max," said Dooley, much relieved, as was I.

"Are you sure it was a he?" I asked.

"He moved like a he," said Dooley.

"But he screamed like a little girl."

Whoever it was, they were gone now, and we could return to the land of nod. Unfortunately, the events had startled us to such an extent we could find sleep no more. And as I lay awake for the rest of the night, I gave myself up to thought about this consortium and its tentacles that seemed to stretch dangerously far and had reached into my own family with an audacity that was simply beyond the pale.

CHAPTER 31

The next morning, bright and early, the four of us were seated on top of the fence, gazing out across Blake's field. In spite of the early hour, dozens of workers were already busily engaged in preparing the field for the work that was to commence. If this was to be the hub of the new Silicon Valley East, I could only imagine the preparations must have been well underway months or perhaps even years ago.

"Isn't that Scarlett's old boyfriend?" asked Brutus, pointing at a sad-looking individual studying a map. "The guy we met yesterday? The architect?"

"Brenton Brooke," said Harriet. "Yeah, that's him. What is he doing here?"

"He's the one who designed the new Town Hall," Brutus explained.

"And who used to date Scarlett," Harriet added. "Very briefly."

We studied the architect as he relayed some of his instructions to the workmen engaged at the site, and then started walking around, looking here and there, possibly trying to envision the site as it should be, based on his plans.

"So he's the one designing this new headquarters," I said.

"Yeah, looks like it," said Harriet. "He looks sick, though."

"Probably suffering from a bad conscience," said Brutus.

As we stood there, a large bird swooped down and we saw how something fell from the bird and landed on the architect's head, who started screaming in dismay. The next moment, an entire flock of birds followed the first bird's example and dive-bombed at the workers on the site and deposited their weapons of muck destruction on the men and women, eliciting howls of confusion and terror from their victims. Diving for cover, it wasn't long before the birds swooped in for a second barrage and then a third. By that time, I guess they ran out of ammunition, and they flew off again, satisfied with the result of their campaign.

The large bird who had led the attack now settled down next to us on the fence. I recognized him as Clark, who had first warned us of impending doom.

"Great job, Clark," I said. "If you can keep this up, you may be able to stop this development."

Clark looked pleased as punch at this compliment. "It's about time that humans start to think about the consequences of their actions," he said. "And trust me, there's a lot more where this came from. I've been rallying the troops, and the boys are extremely motivated."

The workers now gathered near the edge of the field. They didn't look happy as they launched a protest to their foreman and refused to go back to work if their safety wasn't guaranteed. In effect, they went on strike!

"It wasn't just a noxious substance designed to knock out half the population," Clark said. "But also to remove all of the vegetation and plant life in the area. Easier to build an entirely new town if you can get rid of all of the trees and plants and flowers and such. Turn this entire area into one vast wasteland."

"Seems like a short-sighted way of doing things," I said.

"These people aren't exactly the enlightened kind," said Clark.

"How did you learn about their plans?" asked Brutus.

"Pure coincidence. I was resting on a windowsill in Town Hall the other day when I happened to overhear a conversation taking place inside. One of the council members was discussing the plans for the new Hampton Cove with one of his colleagues. Turns out he had received a substantial sum of money to go along with the plans. In exchange, they wouldn't put him in the hospital, like they did with all the other council members and the mayor herself. He's the mayor now."

Ronnie had told us something about an interim mayor, so clearly this was all part of the plan. "Do you think you'll be able to stop this development?" I asked.

Clark shrugged. "We do what we can, but at the end of the day, it's the people who have to decide. Us birds can only do so much. And if they wanted to, they could easily get rid of us by spraying us with some of their poison."

"You're doing a very brave thing, Clark," said Brutus. "Though I can't condone one thing, and that is that you pooped on my human. That was not okay."

Clark grinned. "It's all part of our campaign to make people sit up and think."

"It certainly gave Chase something to think about," said Harriet with a giggle.

Brutus didn't agree, though. "At least it wasn't the birds that spread the toxin."

"How you could ever think that birds could spread any toxin?" said Clark.

"Bird flu!" said Dooley happily. "It's a thing! And it can kill a person."

"Well, I'll tell you right now that I'm a very healthy bird," said Clark.

Clearly, his digestive process was evidence of that, as experienced by the workers employed by the consortium. But Clark was right. There was only so much he and his fellow birds could do. And a bit of poop wouldn't stop construction, but only delay it for a couple of hours. In the end, there was only one thing to be done: Odelia had to reveal the truth about the consortium. That way the conspiracy could be stopped in its tracks once and for all!

The only problem was that we didn't know how high up this conspiracy ran—and who we could trust. And especially: who the ringleader was.

They had already done away with Ronnie and attacked us several times in the last twenty-four hours, so they clearly were prepared to go to extreme lengths to protect their investment and make sure that Hampton Cove was razed to the ground.

CHAPTER 32

Desperate times call for desperate measures, and so it was with some reluctance that I gave my blessing to the plan that Harriet had concocted. This is how we found ourselves back at the hospital, sneaking through its corridors in search of the administrative wing that forms the beating heart of the building.

"Are you sure it's here?" asked Brutus as we slipped through a door marked 'Private.'

"If it's not here, it's over there," said Dooley.

Brutus gave him a stern-faced look. "That makes no sense at all."

"I think it makes perfect sense," said Dooley, and he was probably right.

A voice announced something through the intercom, and we all listened carefully. "I have a feeling we're close," I said. "Very close."

Plenty of people were milling about, always a good sign. Some were dressed in blue smocks, others in green smocks, and still others in white ones.

"What's with all the colors?" asked Brutus.

"It's probably a code," said Dooley. "Like in the army? So they can recognize each other. One color must mean they're higher up in the hierarchy than another."

"I wonder what's highest," Harriet mused. "Blue or green? Or pink or white?"

"It doesn't matter," I said. "Let's focus on the task at hand, shall we?"

And so we trudged on, trying to make sure we weren't seen, which is a lot harder than it sounds. We hid underneath trolleys, and behind doors, and finally thought we had arrived at our destination when a woman sat behind a microphone, sounding a lot like the voice that we had heard over the intercom.

"This is the nerve center!" said Harriet excitedly. "I'm ready, you guys!"

And so were we. So we jumped up onto the table where the woman sat, causing her to emit a scream in surprise. The next moment we jumped down again, with the woman chasing us, since this was one of those places where pets weren't allowed. Behind us, Harriet got ready for the performance of a lifetime.

ODELIA HAD EXPERIENCED a fitful night's sleep and was suffering from a terrible headache. She'd told one of the nurses, who had given her something for the pain, and even though she was feeling a little better, clearly whatever had knocked her out the day before was still in her system and hadn't fully been flushed out. The doctors couldn't tell them what it was, only that it had affected half the population of Hampton Cove, so it must have been something potent.

Judging by her pounding head, they didn't have to

convince her of that. Next to her, Chase had also woken up and looked as bedraggled as she was feeling.

"How are you, babe?" he asked.

"Headache," she murmured.

"Same here," he said weakly.

"And me," said Uncle Alec, one bed over.

"Me too," said Charlene.

"It must be the drugs they gave us," said Mom.

"I feel fine," said Dad. "Fit as a fiddle."

Odelia smiled. "Of course you do, Dad."

She hoped they would be allowed to leave today. Even though she wasn't ready to go back to work, she seriously wanted to go home. According to the doctor, the fact that they had woken up was a minor miracle, and he couldn't understand why they would be the only ones who had reversed the effects of whatever had put them in a coma in the first place.

She could have explained to him about the potency of Harriet's vocal cords, but he wouldn't have believed her, so she chose not to say.

The television that hung suspended in a corner of the room had brought them up to date on the events as they had unfolded over the course of the last twenty-four hours, with lots of people contracting this mysterious illness and being taken to the hospital. The CDC had been brought in to investigate, and to determine if they were the only ones affected or if the virus or disease was likely to spread.

It wasn't too much to say that a panic had set in, and that those who hadn't landed in the hospital had opted to move away from Hampton Cove for the time being, hoping that would safeguard them from ending up in the hospital themselves.

That morning she had held a long phone call with Gran, who had finally brought her up to speed on what was really going on behind the scenes. The story had caused the hairs on the back of her neck to stand at attention. Planes dumping toxic waste on inhabitants? The water supply being poisoned? Political shenanigans going on behind the scenes? And most importantly, their town about to be wiped off the map, all so a couple of people could become outrageously rich?

It sounded like the scenario for a bad Hollywood blockbuster, but it was happening right here, right now, in their own pleasant little hamlet!

She had informed the others, and the moment she had, Charlene had picked up the phone and called her former council member—now acting mayor—but he had been evasive and reassuring, which spelled trouble with a capital T.

Most likely, she said, the guy was in on it.

Just then, there was a crackle from the intercom located in a corner of the room, and all of a sudden a familiar screeching sound burst through the speaker. It cut through Odelia like a knife, and as she pressed her hands to her ears, she knew what this meant. The cats were trying to repeat the procedure that had been instrumental in waking up their humans from their coma the day before. Only this time, they were using the hospital's intercom system to reach everybody. And if the vigor and volume of Harriet's caterwauling was any indication, it wouldn't be long before every single patient was awake and clamoring for earplugs. After all, the noise the Persian produced was so dreadful it might very well raise the dead!

CHAPTER 33

For the time being, and while Harriet did her thing, we decided to wait things out in our humans' room, where we would be safe from any nosy hospital administrators or overzealous nurses. And so we slipped into the room and hopped onto Odelia's bed, taking refuge underneath her bedsheets.

Harriet's recital had just reached its fever pitch when the door to the hospital room opened again and a male nurse strode in, carrying a tray, as is often the case in hospitals, with a series of syringes placed on it.

"Time for your medicine," he announced in that faux chipper voice that nurses learn in nursing school.

"Oh, not again," Uncle Alec groaned unhappily.

"I'm sure we don't need any more medicine," Chase chimed in.

"Yeah, the doc told us we're allowed to go home today," said Odelia.

"Just a precaution," said the nurse, placing down the tray and preparing the first syringe. "We wouldn't want to suffer a relapse now, would we?"

For some odd reason, the voice of this nurse suddenly sounded familiar to me, and so I decided to take a closer look at the medicine slinger and syringe officiant. Imagine my surprise when I found that I was face to face with... Ronnie Vincent!

For a moment, I found myself unable to speak. Now why would Ronnie, who until that moment was presumed captured by the consortium and possibly dead, have suddenly decided on a change of career and found gainful employment as a nurse? It didn't seem to make a lot of sense. Until I caught a whiff of his cologne.

Musky with a hint of lemon. Just like our nocturnal marauder!

"Don't let him stick that needle in you, Odelia," I said urgently.

"What?" said Odelia, much surprised.

But the 'nurse' had caught sight of me, and didn't like what he saw.

"Cats are not allowed in here," he said. "We have strict policies about that. I'm afraid I'll have to get rid of him."

"You're not getting rid of my cat," said Odelia.

But Ronnie was already grabbing me by the lapels—or rather the scruff of the neck—and carting me off in the direction of the door—when Dooley poked his head out.

"Hey, you can't take my friend!" he cried.

"Another one," Ronnie growled, and took a hold of Dooley as well.

"What's going on?" asked Brutus, also popping up like a jack-in-the-box.

"God, this place is infested with the creatures!" cried Ronnie.

"He's a bad one, Odelia," I cried. "He broke into our home last night, looking through your stuff. And if I'm not mistaken, he's on the consortium payroll!"

And so while Ronnie struggled to contain this 'cat infestation,' Odelia decided to climb out of bed and take matters into her own hands. She was a little weak-kneed, which was only to be expected after what she had been through, but still determined to save us from this whistleblower who wasn't a whistleblower at all.

"Put my cats down," she said in firm tones. "Right now!"

The man plastered a fake smile on his face. "Now, now. You shouldn't be out of bed, young lady."

"Put them down!" she repeated, pointing to the floor to make her meaning perfectly clear.

"It's just cats," said Chase from the next bed. "They can't do any harm."

"Yeah, my niece is very attached to those cats," said Uncle Alec. "So you better do as she says or she will write a nasty piece about you." He grinned, and seemed to find the whole thing extremely hilarious.

"It's true that we should probably follow hospital procedure," said Tex, always a stickler for medical protocol. "Have those cats been properly sanitized?"

Marge gave her husband a scathing look. "Are you calling our cats dirty?"

"No, no, of course not," Tex hastened to say. "Just not very clean, you see."

"Our cats aren't dirty," Marge insisted. "And I say they can stay."

"Cats have a very positive impact on patients suffering from a disease," said Charlene, putting her two cents out there. "It's been proven time and again."

Ronnie, who could see the way the wind was blowing, decided to put us down. "Just this once, all right? But don't let the doctor see them or he'll kick them out for sure."

"Odelia, this man is a bad egg," I told her urgently. "So I

wouldn't let him stick that needle in you. He's bound to put you all back to sleep!"

Odelia nodded as a sign she had understood.

"What's in those syringes, exactly?" she asked.

"Oh, just some stimulants," said Ronnie airily as he returned to preparing the first injection. "Only good stuff to get you back on your feet in no time."

"We have been okayed by the doctor to leave today," said Charlene. She smiled. "And frankly I can't wait to go back to work. Things have been pretty hectic out there if I'm not mistaken."

"It certainly has been challenging," Ronnie agreed as he approached Odelia. "Just a little sting," he said.

"Not today," said Odelia, and slapped the needle from the man's hand!

"Odelia!" said Uncle Alec, shocked. "What are you doing!"

"She has always been like this," said Tex. "As a child she was quite willful."

"It must be the coma she was in," Marge added. "Odelia, you will apologize to the nurse right now."

"Mom, Dad," said Odelia. "This man isn't a real nurse." She was pointing to a stunned-looking Ronnie now. "His name is Ronnie Vincent and he works for the consortium that's turning Hampton Cove into a ghost town."

"What are you talking about?" said Ronnie, smiling uncertainly. "Of course I'm a nurse. I've worked here for years. And if you don't take that medicine now, I'm afraid you might suffer a relapse. And we don't want that now, do we?"

The other members of Odelia's family were in a quandary about how to proceed. And I could see their point. From their perspective, Odelia was simply being a difficult patient, possibly as a consequence of some form of delirium brought on by the disease that had put them all in the hospital in the first place.

"Marge, this man is a crook," said Brutus. "So you better grab a hold of him and make sure he can't get away."

"But I thought he was one of the good guys?" said Dooley.

"He's not," I said determinedly. "He works for the same people who ran us off the road last night and shot at us, and who knocked out Scarlett yesterday, and who spread that noxious airborne gas that put half this town in the hospital."

Marge had been listening carefully, even as the fake nurse approached Odelia with the syringe, eager to give her the jab.

"Alec, this man is a crook," she said now.

Uncle Alec seemed stunned by this sudden change of mind in his sister. But quickly determining that if both Marge and Odelia sang the same tune, it must come from their cats, and knowing from long association with us that we were often right on the money, he hoisted himself up, climbed out of bed and placed a heavy hand on the nurse. "Sir, you're under arrest for impersonating a nurse."

Ronnie stared at the policeman for a moment, then suddenly jabbed that needle into the man's chest with all his might, pushed down on the plunger and as Uncle Alec reeled and staggered back, broke into a run and made for the exit.

Which is when he happened to stumble over Dooley, who had strategically taken up position right behind the guy, and he went down hard.

Chase, who doesn't like it when people threaten his wife with injections and certainly not when they attack his boss, now jumped out of bed and descended on the guy, pinning him to the floor.

Charlene or one of the others must have pushed the bell alerting the real nurses, for three of them now came hurrying into the room, and when they saw Chase sitting atop one of their own, they were for a moment stunned. The fact that all of those present in the room were talking across one another didn't help. But finally Chase managed to pierce the noise by yelling, "He injected my boss with some poison!"

"But... he's not a nurse," said one of the nurses as she studied the man.

But then their training kicked in, and they immediately flocked to Uncle Alec, who was lying on the floor, breathing a little shallowly, and not looking his best.

"What did you use!" one of the nurses demanded of Ronnie Vincent.

But the former whistleblower decided to plead the fifth.

CHAPTER 34

*J*ust then, Gran and Scarlett walked in, both carrying bouquets of flowers for the patients. When they saw the strange scene, with one nurse being held down by Chase and other nurses surrounding a seemingly unresponsive Uncle Alec on the floor, Gran immediately dropped the flowers and hurried to her son's side.

"What's wrong?" she cried. "Tell me!"

"This man injected him with something," said one of the nurses. "But he refuses to tell us what it is."

Gran slowly turned to Ronnie Vincent. "You did this?" she asked.

"He works for the consortium, Gran," I said.

"And he broke into our house last night," Dooley added.

"Yeah, I recognized his cologne," I explained.

"He's been playing us for a bunch of fools," Brutus growled.

Gran now rolled up her sleeves and descended upon the man who had put her son out of commission. She got up close and personal, menace clear in her voice. "You're going to tell me what you injected into my son," she said. "Or else I won't be held responsible for the consequences—is that understood!"

Ronnie, who hadn't been impressed by Chase's threats, seemed a little scared now. But he still wasn't prepared to give us anything. Instead, he opted to remain mum.

"We'll have these checked by the lab," said one of the nurses as she picked up the syringes that had fallen to the floor. "Hopefully, we'll be able to find out what's in them and work out an antidote."

Harriet, back from her successful mission, now strode into the room. "They're all awake!" she announced. "I checked a few of the rooms, and everyone is waking up from their coma! Who knew there were so many art lovers in Hampton Cove?" But when she became aware of the scene of turmoil, she forgot all about her triumph. "What's wrong with Uncle Alec? Did he take a turn for the worse? And what is Ronnie Vincent doing here? Does he have more bad news to share?"

In a few brief words, we brought her up to date on the latest events as they had transpired. When she learned of Uncle Alec's fate, her face fell. "Oh, no!" she said. "But he can't do that!"

"Well, he did," said Brutus. "And now he's refusing to tell us what he used."

Harriet walked up to Uncle Alec, shed a single tear for the fallen police chief, and, possibly out of sheer habit, or because of the wealth of emotion welling up inside her, burst into song once more. It didn't take more than a few bars for the policeman to stir and open his eyes. "Not that horrible racket again!" he cried.

"You, sir," said Harriet, much insulted, "are a cultural barbarian!"

Ronnie Vincent looked on, surprise written all over his

features. "That's impossible," he said. "That stuff should have knocked him out for hours!"

"What did you give him?" asked Chase. "Tell us!"

And as the man accepted defeat, he said, "Rohypnol."

"I feel a little woozy," said Uncle Alec as he touched his head.

But then Gran was giving him a big hug, and Charlene was showering him with a thousand kisses, and his sister was helping him up. Before long, the Chief was back in bed, with hospital staff hovering around him with tender care.

* * *

Interim Mayor Weston Pilbrow had been going over some of the building applications his paymasters had given him to sign. He had already rubberstamped most of them and only had a few dozen more to go when all of a sudden the door to his office burst open, and Charlene Butterwick walked in, accompanied by that burly detective Kingsley and three other police officers.

"Charlene!" he said, employing his most unctuous tone. "What a pleasant surprise!"

"Not very pleasant for me," said Charlene, who looked all business and also, Weston had to admit, not as sick as she should have been. According to the information he had received, she should have been at death's door, knocked out for at least a couple more weeks.

He walked from behind his desk, hands outstretched. But instead of gripping his offered hand and shaking it, Detective Kingsley suddenly produced a pair of handcuffs out of thin air and placed them on his wrists!

"Weston Pilbrow," said the detective. "You're under arrest!"

"Charlene?" he asked. "What's the meaning of this?"

"I'm assuming control again, Weston," she said. "Effective immediately, you're no longer interim mayor. We have reason to suspect you've been working with a secret cabal to sell out this entire town and turn it into one gigantic industrial park. The hub, in fact, of something called Silicon Valley East, which is supposed to comprise all of Long Island, effectively driving out our local inhabitants."

"Not all the inhabitants," Weston sputtered in protest. "Some of them are welcome to stay, of course. If they fit the right profile. We'll be needing lots of engineers, computer technicians…" He gave her a keen look. "Don't you want to put this town on the map, Charlene? Hampton Cove will become the hub of the new Silicon Valley East. The capital of the entire region. It's going to be the most exciting and ambitious project we've both been involved in. And isn't that why we went into politics in the first place? To get things done? To change the world?"

"Not if it means destroying hundreds of local communities," said Charlene curtly. "Simply so a couple of outrageously rich people can become even outrageously richer." She turned to the detective. "Take him away, Chase."

"You won't be able to reverse this, you know," said Weston. "These people are a lot more powerful than you can imagine. And they've got friends in high places."

But Charlene wasn't impressed. "Just get him out of my sight," she said.

He was surprised to find that when he exited Town Hall and was led to a police vehicle, dozens of other people were also being led away. He recognized them as loyal civil servants—loyal to him, that is, not Charlene. He hung his head. It looked like the consortium had been dealt a serious blow.

CHAPTER 35

The four of us were resting peacefully on the porch swing, feeling we had deserved a respite from the events that had engulfed our town. Charlene had been reinstalled at Town Hall, doing what she could to reverse the decisions her replacement had made, Uncle Alec had rounded up members of the conspiracy at a rapid pace, following certain revelations that Ronnie had made. The man who had presented himself as a whistleblower on the consortium had finally found his true calling: as a whistleblower on the consortium. And Odelia had been writing up a storm, publishing article after article on the conspiracy that had put up to fifty percent of our town's population in the hospital.

The impact of her articles resonated around the country, and even the FBI had started their investigations and had been busy building a case against the people behind the whole sordid affair—members of the East Coast business community who had seen an opportunity to replicate the impressive success of Silicon Valley but had failed to take into consideration that it would wreak havoc on millions of people, destroy their homes, and cause mass disruption to an entire region.

Next to me, Dooley also enjoyed a pleasant nap, and so did Harriet and Brutus. It wasn't too much to say that we had played our small part in thwarting the conspiracy and warding off the danger that had almost turned our home to rubble and forced us to relocate to some other part of the country. I happen to like Hampton Cove, and I wouldn't have enjoyed pulling up stakes and starting over.

A large bird now settled down next to us. I glanced up at the bird. "Hey, Clark."

"Max," said the raven. "So it looks as if our mission is over, huh?"

"Looks like it," I said. "Unless you enjoy pooping on people so much you want to continue?"

He smiled. "Not really. It's a big hassle. Though I've gotten pretty good at it. I almost never miss these days."

"I can't imagine it's easy to hit a person," I said.

"Oh, you have no idea," said the black raven. "You have to account for velocity, wind speed, temperature, height. It takes a lot of skill to do it right." He sighed a wistful sigh. "And the satisfaction you derive is out of this world. When you land a perfectly aimed poo on a person's head—there's simply nothing like it."

"I think people got the message," I said. "And if it hadn't been for you, Hampton Cove would probably have ceased to exist. So from the bottom of my heart: thank you, Clark."

"You're welcome, Max. And I have to say: if you hadn't picked up the ball and run with it, I wouldn't have been able to accomplish much. These people weren't going to let a couple of pooping birds stand in their way. I'm sure they already had plans to start dumping their toxic waste on us, eradicating the local bird population and getting rid of us for good."

"That would have been a terrible decision. Without birds and bugs and plants and nature in general, where are we? Living in some concrete jungle. No, thanks."

"Well, anyway, I wanted to express my gratitude for the way you handled this, Max. And if you ever need my help—"

"Well, there's this lawyer," I said. "He goes by the name of Levi Kidner?"

Clark smiled. "I remember him well. He works for the consortium, just like the others. Only he got cold feet, and so the consortium decided to teach him a lesson by breaking into his office. I think he got the message, for he soon left town."

"You really had your eye on the ball, didn't you? You saw what was happening way before anyone else did."

"Birds have the bird's eye view, Max. We know."

"I know you do," I said.

"The only one who escaped our attention was Ronnie Vincent. I really thought he was one of the good guys."

"That was the role he'd been asked to play. As the whistleblower who goes around rallying people against the plans of the consortium. While, in actual fact, he was their local leader and worked tirelessly to identify anyone who might pose a threat and then sent his goons to intimidate them to give up their opposition."

Dooley, who had been listening intently, said, "That was a very clever plan."

"It was," I said. "We all fell for his act. And so he knew exactly who opposed the plans of his bosses and also knew how to get rid of them."

"He almost got rid of us," Brutus grunted unhappily.

"They hadn't counted on our secret weapon," I said.

We all looked at Harriet, who stretched luxuriously and yawned. "Are you talking about me? I can feel it when people are talking about me. I get this tingle at the back of my neck."

She smiled. "It was so much fun to perform in front of a live audience of hundreds of adoring fans. Even if they were comatose."

"Even better," said Clark. "That way they couldn't escape!"

I wanted to laugh, but when I saw Harriet's expression, I didn't.

Harriet launched a dirty look at the raven. "You're not funny, Clark."

"I'm sorry," said Clark. "You did a great thing. If it hadn't been for you, those people would still be in a coma right now, and we would be in big trouble."

It certainly had been a master stroke to get rid of the mayor and all the council members who might oppose the consortium's plans, as well as the chief of police and countless others who could stand in their way. And once they finally woke up, they would wake up in a different world. A world that would have changed beyond recognition. In other words, we'd all had a narrow escape!

Clark flew off as more people arrived: Scarlett, Uncle Alec and Charlene, Wilbur Vickery, and even Father Reilly had decided to grace us with his presence. As a consequence, the porch got a little busy with the addition of Clarice, Shanille, and Kingman, all eager to partake in the great feast Tex was laying out for his guests. Like probably everyone in Hampton Cove, the doctor was extremely grateful for the work that the watch had been instrumental in and also its feline equivalent, and so he decided to dig deep and offer us some of his tastiest bits.

"So what's going to happen to Blake's field?" asked Kingman as he sniffed the air with anticipatory relish.

"Well, Blake sold the field to the consortium," I said. "So he doesn't own it anymore. But since there will be a trial, and the consortium will probably be officially disbanded and its possessions confiscated, I guess Blake's field will belong to the government—either local or state or federal."

"I hope they'll turn it into a park," said Shanille. "We could even use it for our rehearsals."

"And I hope they leave it as is," said Clarice. "A derelict field like that is heaven for rats, and we all know how healthy a good fat rat is for any cat." When none of us shared her excitement, she added, "Plenty of protein and fiber!"

"Absolutely, Clarice," said Shanille, but her endorsement lacked the ring of conviction.

Clarice sniffed the air. "Ooh, some tasty stuff is heading our way!"

"And it's not rats," Dooley pointed out, much to Clarice's amusement.

And as our stomachs grumbled, Rufus came trotting up from next door. He didn't look entirely pleased. "Hey, you guys," he said in sad tones.

"What's wrong, Rufus?" asked Harriet. "Hasn't Ted been feeding you?"

"Oh, he has been feeding me," Rufus assured us, referring to the one cardinal rule no pet owner should ever sin against. "But I can tell his heart isn't in it."

"He was really hoping to get that job, wasn't he?" I said.

Rufus nodded. "Much as it pains me to admit it, both Ted and Marcie were all on board with this consortium's evil designs on our lovely little town. They were sold hook, line, and sinker. And the fact that the consortium was busted means Ted will have to go and find a new job."

"That shouldn't be a problem," said Kingman. "Accountants are always in great demand."

"Yeah, someone needs to count all of that money shopkeepers make," said Shanille, cutting a look at Kingman, who took it in stride.

"I'll have you know that Wilbur doesn't make as much

money as you all seem to think," the voluminous cat professed. "In fact, he barely makes ends meet sometimes. With local taxes, state taxes, and federal taxes, it's a miracle he can manage to put three square meals a day on the table at all!"

And as he launched into a long diatribe about the hardships a small business owner faces, I focused on Tex and his ministrations behind the grill for a moment, not all that interested in Wilbur's lamentations. It wasn't long before Odelia came up to us with plenty of goodies in store, and doled them out with abject pleasure.

"Here," she said as she filled our bowls to our heart's content. "You deserve it. If it hadn't been for you and the watch, I would probably still be in the hospital right now." She patted Harriet's head. "And I've got an extra-special treat for our star." And she placed some delicious little nugget in front of a delighted Harriet.

And as we all dug in, and even Kingman stopped complaining about the taxman, Odelia raised her voice. "Let's give a warm applause to our heroes," she said. "The watch—and the cats!"

Loud cheers rang out, and Harriet even got up and took a bow.

"Oh, you guys," she said breathlessly. "This is my proudest moment. To know that I've saved the world with my art. It's the best feeling in the world."

"Rumor has it that they've made a recording of your singing," said Shanille. "And that they will play it for their most difficult coma patients. Is this true?"

"Absolutely," said Harriet. "I had to sit down and do several takes, and they got it all on tape, and they said they'll use it on their most hopeless cases. Isn't that just great? Imagine being in a coma for years, and suddenly to be awakened to the sound of a beautiful song? It must be like floating on the wings of heaven."

"More like descending into an inferno of auditory purgatory," Clarice murmured, earning herself a searing look from Harriet.

"As I keep saying, the world is full of art barbarians," she said prissily.

But since the food was delicious, and we had just achieved a major victory against the forces of darkness, no more words of strife or disagreement followed, and as we all basked in the atmosphere of camaraderie, soon the time came to take a nice long nap and let those gastric juices work their magic and enjoy a feast of their own.

"Max?" asked Dooley.

"Mh?" I said.

"Why do you think Gran wasn't put into a coma, along with the others?"

"Because the consortium didn't consider her a threat," I said. "Apparently they had a cut-off age of sixty and didn't want to bother with anyone above that age. The poison they spread was specifically engineered that way."

"They should have thought twice," said my friend.

"Yeah, I guess that was their fatal mistake."

"So… do you think it's safe to drink the water?"

I smiled. "Perfectly safe, Dooley. I wouldn't worry about it."

In fact, the water plant had put something in the drinking water to counteract the effect of the poison the consortium had spread in the air, making sure that every last residue was washed out of people's systems. And a much more stringent safety procedure had been adopted to ensure that the water couldn't be tampered with in the future. They had caught us sleeping at the wheel once, but that wouldn't happen a second time—not if Charlene had a say in it.

The sound of tinkling cutlery and babbling voices lulled me into a pleasant sleep, and before long, I was dreaming of soft meadows of grass that tickled my belly and birds chirping pleasantly, flowers spreading their delicious scent, bees buzzing happily, and in general nature giving of its best.

Which is when all of a sudden, the sound of a buzz saw cut through my naptime and made me wake up with a jolt. As I looked around in search of the source of the terrible noise, I saw that Harriet had decided to regale us with a medley of her greatest hits. And as she gave me a wink, she said, "An ounce of prevention is worth a pound of cure, Max. So just sit back and relax—and let yourself be healed!"

Unfortunately for her, our humans didn't ascribe to her point of view, and before long, Marge simply picked the pretty Persian prima donna up from the porch, placed her inside the house, closed the door, and locked the pet flap.

Fame. It *is* a fickle food.

THE END

Thanks for reading! If you want to know when a new Nic Saint book comes out, sign up for Nic's mailing list: nicsaint.com/news

EXCERPT FROM PURRFECT GUITAR (MAX 80)

Chapter One

Luke Boynes picked up the small nosegay of flowers he had purchased and wondered if it would suffice. He had been pondering popping the big question since his first date with Molly. It was love at first sight, at least on his part, but he wasn't sure the feeling was entirely reciprocal. His best friend Sam had told him in no uncertain terms he was a fool if he didn't gird his loins and do the right thing. All he had to do was screw up his courage, get it over with, and very soon the wedding bells would ring out, and they'd all be able to put their feet under the table at the appropriate venue, and Sam could finally brush up on his oratory skills and deliver the best man speech he knew he had in him.

Luke wasn't so sure, though. The last time he'd seen Molly, she hadn't been as keen as she could have been on being cloistered with him for the duration of the evening. In fact, she had been disappointingly distracted by her phone, which led him to believe that those warm feelings she may have harbored at the outset of their acquaintance had already cooled down considerably.

It was the curse of the Boynes. At the first meeting, any potential partner they met would be over the moon with delight, but that initial excitement wouldn't last, and before long, the fire died, and what was left were the faint feelings of what could have been but never would. It had been thus for his big brother Jackson, still pining for the girl who got away fifteen years ago, or their sister Margery, whose prince charming had ultimately found love and happiness in the arms of another woman. Even their mom and pop had only found each other after many wrong turns and botched matches. But at least they did find each other, which was more than could be said about their unfortunate offspring, still chomping at the bit to get to the starting line.

He wandered into the venue he had selected for his lunch date with Molly and admired the scenery, which mainly consisted of many hopefuls just like himself, wining and dining their sweethearts to within an inch of their lives, eyes locked on the target while murmuring those sweet nothings that made all the difference. All in all, it lifted his heart to such an extent he felt a glimmer of hope that today would be the day. The day he would be able to link his lot to the most lovely woman on the face of the planet and possibly the universe.

So he took a deep breath, announced to the maître d' that he had reserved a table for two and was immediately brought to the spot in question, where he proceeded to await the arrival of the party of the second part—Molly Ashmore.

It wasn't long before he started to wonder if she had read his messages, for even twenty minutes into the proceedings, the woman was still a no-show. Just when he was thinking that all his hopes would be dashed and he had fallen victim to the Boynes curse once again, suddenly the russet curly head of the only girl in the world made itself seen entering the premises and glancing hither and thither in search of the man who had swept her off her feet—or at least had made a valiant attempt at doing so.

Molly looked radiant as always—tonight perhaps a little more so than usual—though it could also be Luke's prejudice, as the glasses he was wearing had suddenly been substituted for the kind of rose-tinted ones your true lover likes to wear on these occasions. He felt his pocket for the ring box he had concealed there for the *moment suprême*, swallowed away the lump of unease that seemed to have permanently taken up position in his throat, thereby dislodging the mint that he had stuck under his tongue and gulping it down. He got up to greet the lady in question. Only when he made to greet her in the ebullient fashion he knew was *de rigueur* on these occasions, instead of heading straight to his table and settling down, she made a beeline for a nearby table instead. As he watched on in a sort of stupefied manner, his jaw dropping a couple of inches out of sheer perturbation, he saw she was greeted by a young man who looked awfully familiar to him. And as the couple shared a smile, his foggy brain trying to grasp what was going on, one thing did penetrate: instead of writing his best man's speech as he should be doing, Sam had been wooing the girl Luke had earmarked for his own. For it was indeed his best friend who now took Molly's hand and proceeded to lovingly gaze into those wonderful eyes!

Adding insult to injury, Molly gazed right back and seemed to like it too!

It was, in other words, a broken Luke Boynes who staggered out of the restaurant, his ring still in his pocket, his song unsung, his roseate dreams unfulfilled and his heart at the bottom of the canal he set out to drown himself and his sorrows in. In due course he arrived at his destination, and he would have jumped in if not another man had beaten him to the punch. And when he looked a little closer, he saw this man looked very dead indeed, which gave him a feeling foul play might be involved here. And since he was essentially a law-abiding citizen, even when his heart had just been ripped to shreds by the two people he thought most of in this world, he took out his phone and called it in.

Even he could see that his own plight wasn't as bad as that of the waterlogged person floating in the canal. He may have had a symbolic knife plunged into his back by his best friend, but at least he was still alive and breathing, while this poor sucker was obviously as dead as a dodo.

And so he sank down on a nearby bench and awaited further proceedings.

Chapter Two

I had been studying a snail who had decided to make our lawn its new home when a sound alerted me that important developments were imminent. The snail moved at a snail's pace, which is par for the course with these creatures, and as a consequence my attention had waned. So this distraction in the form of Odelia emerging from the house and calling out my name was welcome.

"Max, there's been a murder. Let's go," she said in that crisp, businesslike tone she likes to adopt when the call comes in. More often than not, the person on the other side of that call is her uncle, chief of police of the lovely hamlet we live in, and also more often than not, the tidings he brings are not of the kind to bring a song of joy to one's lips. Our hamlet may be small and lovely, but that doesn't mean it is entirely devoid of the criminal aspect. Even in paradise, a snake will eagerly slither about, its perniciousness to perform. Such is the case that many a murder has taken place in Hampton Cove of late, and since Odelia is married to a policeman and is a policeman's niece, more often than not her expertise is called upon to assist in tackling these cases. And since she happens to be in a position to rope me and my friends into those inquiries, we gladly comply.

"What's going on, Max?" asked Dooley now—my best friend and wingcat.

"I'm not sure," I said. "Odelia says there's been a murder."

"Oh, no!" said Dooley, who is a peaceable type of cat and doesn't appreciate it when people go about murdering other people. "Who's the victim?"

"No idea," I said as I got to my paws and stretched.

Like me, Dooley had been resting peacefully on the lawn, allowing grass to tickle his belly and generally taking a load off his paws. At the bottom of the garden, something stirred underneath the rose bushes, and the sound of a giggle gave us an indication as to who might be causing those stirrings.

"Harriet! Brutus!" I yelled, therefore. "Duty calls!"

A furry face popped out from between the roses. It belonged to Harriet, the white Persian not looking all that happy about this rude interruption.

"What is it this time?" she asked with a touch of annoyance.

"Murder," I said in what I hoped was an appropriately grave tone.

She rolled her eyes. "Again? Maybe you can handle this one, Max?"

Now it was my turn to turn a little censorious. "You know the drill, Harriet."

"Oh, for Pete's sakes," she said, and for a moment, I fully expected her to blatantly refuse to play ball. But then she emerged from her favorite bushes, her boyfriend Brutus in tow.

"I'm not sure I signed up for this," said the butch black cat.

EXCERPT FROM PURRFECT GUITAR (MAX 80)

"When did I sign up for this? Cause if I did, I must have been suffering a lapse of judgment."

"You signed up for this when you moved in," I said with a smile.

I could fully understand where he was coming from. After all, cats aren't usually dragged along on these investigative outings by their humans. But then Odelia isn't a regular person. She's the kind of person who can talk to cats, just like her mother and grandmother and all of their forebears—a gift handed down the generations from mother to daughter. A genetic quirk, if you will, that has made Odelia the most sought-after reporter in town since she can always be relied upon to dig out the most insignificant clue and link it to the investigation. All because we hand her those clues on a platter, since cats are the perfect sleuths. Always ready to bring our inquisitive minds to bear on any mystery, and capable of talking to other pets and get them to spill the beans.

"And here I thought I'd lead a perfectly peaceful life," Brutus grumbled. "But instead I'm being dragged from crime scene to crime scene with nary a respite."

"Oh, I'm sure it's not that bad," I said. "How long has it been since we were called in to assist in some murder or other crime? Must be weeks."

"It's easy enough for you," said Harriet, joining her boyfriend in voicing his qualms about the tasks that had been awarded to us by Odelia and her family. "With that big brain of yours, you solve these murders in a heartbeat. It's much harder for us, not having been blessed with a sixth sense when it comes to sniffing out clues and chasing suspects. Oftentimes I feel we're simply along for the ride. Nothing but a sideshow. Bit players you can bounce your ideas off of."

"You know that's not true," I said, aghast at these accusations. "I'm sure Odelia appreciates your input as much as she does mine. Probably more, in fact."

Harriet preened a little. "You're just saying that to make me feel better."

"No, I'm not!" I said emphatically. "We're all in this together, and Odelia couldn't do this without you, Harriet. Or you, Brutus. Or Dooley, of course."

"My ideas are always very good," said Dooley proudly. "The best, in fact."

Now even Brutus was grinning. "Aren't they just?"

"I still feel we should be given a bigger role in Odelia's investigations from now on," said Harriet, not prepared to let her grievance be dismissed so easily. "I daresay Brutus and I should be allowed to take the lead, not you."

"Fine with me," I said. As long as we got a move on, I was ready to agree with any of her demands, even if I wasn't entirely sure she'd be prepared to put her money where her mouth was.

She stared at me. "Are you sure about that, Max?"

"Absolutely," I said. "If you want to take the lead on this investigation, be my guest. I'll take a backseat, and you won't hear a single peep from me."

She smiled. "That's exactly what I wanted to hear, Max." She turned to her mate. "Snuggle bug, from now on we're in charge. So let's crack this case like no case has ever been cracked!"

And so she charged forward and disappeared into the house.

Brutus gave me a helpless look. "Max, are you sure this is a good idea?"

"Absolutely," I said. "If Harriet wants to take the lead, I say let her."

He sighed. "Oh, boy. I have a feeling we're in for a bumpy ride!"

Chapter Three

When Odelia arrived at the location her uncle had specified over the phone, she found both the Chief and her husband Chase in situ, as well as Abe Cornwall, the county coroner, who was busily inspecting the waterlogged corpse that had been dragged from the canal. Apparently, the body had gone into the canal at some point before the McMillan Street lock and had been prevented from being swept along further, which was just as well, as it may otherwise have ended up in the ocean, never to be found.

"So what do we have?" she asked as she knelt down next to Abe.

The fizzy-haired coroner gave her an appreciative look. "Aren't we in a good mood today? What's the occasion, if I may ask?"

She smiled. "No particular occasion." That wasn't entirely true, though. Since she and Chase had been married now for a year, they had planned to celebrate the occasion by going away on their own to New England and spend the weekend at a great little hotel they had found online. Her mom would take care of Grace, and it would be just the two of them for one long weekend. She couldn't wait to leave and had been looking forward to it for weeks.

"Okay, so this man is dead," said the coroner, getting down to business.

"I can see that," Uncle Alec grunted. "But what made him this way is what I would like to know."

"Well, that's a little hard to ascertain just from looking at him," said Abe as he studied the mortal remains of the man a little closely. "He suffered some bumps and bruises, but whether those were sustained before he fell into the canal or after is something I'll have to determine once I get him on my slab."

"So he could simply have stumbled into the canal on his

own?" asked Chase, who stood wide-legged and arms crossed as he stoically surveyed the scene.

"That's exactly right, detective," said Abe.

"So no foul play?" asked Uncle Alec.

"Not that I can determine at first glance."

Uncle Alec immediately perked up to a great degree. "Well, that's that then," he said, much buoyed by this information. "Accidental death. Makes life a lot easier for us, that's for sure." He turned to his niece. "I'm sorry to drag you out like this, honey. But when the call came in, I thought there'd been a murder."

"There could still have been a murder," said Abe, deciding to rain on the police chief's parade. "What I'm saying is that it's too soon to tell." He gave Uncle Alec a meaningful look, causing the latter to bridle a little.

"But you said…"

"I said that at first glance I can't find any sign of foul play. But that doesn't mean it's not there." He got up with a slight creaking of the knees. "I'll know more once I've done a post-mortem. In the meantime, perhaps you can try and find out who this poor man is and how he ended up here?" He gave them a fine smile. "That is, after all, part of your job description?" And with these words, he bid them adieu and gave his team the go-ahead to remove the body from the scene.

"What did he mean by that?" Chief Alec asked.

"He meant that we shouldn't jump to conclusions," said Chase as he rubbed his chin. "Who called it in?"

Uncle Alec gestured to a forlorn figure seated on a bench nearby. And so Odelia and Chase walked up to the man, whose name turned out to be Luke Boynes, and who looked a little shell-shocked, as was only to be expected.

"I didn't see him at first," said Mr. Boynes. "And then when I did, I thought he had fallen in, so I…" He gulped a little as he thought back to the terrible moment he had come upon the dead man.

"You did a good thing there, Mr. Boynes," said Chase as he placed an encouraging hand on the man's shoulder. "Many would have walked away."

"How did you happen to be here, if I may ask?" said Odelia.

"Oh, I just wanted to go for a walk," said Mr. Boynes. "Clear my head, you know." When they both waited for more information, he relented. "I had arranged to meet a woman in a restaurant, but as it turned out, she stood me up. So I..." He turned a sad look in the direction of the canal, and Odelia thought she saw all. Could it be that this man had intended to take his own life but had changed his mind after he saw that floater? Her keen reporter's mind sensed that there might be a story here, but that this wasn't the right time to pursue it. She still filed it away in the back of her mind for later use. Once Mr. Boynes had recovered from the shock, she'd have another little chat.

"Let's get you home," said Chase. "Where do you live, Mr. Boynes?"

The man gave them a feeble smile. "Luke, please. And you don't have to go to any trouble on my account, detective. I can make my own way home."

"Nonsense," said Chase determinedly. "After the shock you had, you shouldn't be driving home all by yourself. Do you live alone, sir?"

Luke nodded sadly. "I do, yeah. Unfortunately."

As he got up, a ring box fell from his pocket. Odelia picked it up and glanced inside. It was a neat little bauble, and any girl would be happy to receive it. She closed the box and handed it to the sad-looking man. "I believe this is yours?"

With a touch of embarrassment, he took it from her hand

and tucked it away. "I won't be needing that anymore," he murmured, and then they handed him over to one of Chase's officers who would escort him home and make sure he got there safe and sound and wouldn't be left to his own devices after the ordeal he'd suffered. All part of the 'job description,' as Abe would have said.

They watched as the body of the drowning victim was placed on a stretcher and tucked into a waiting ambulance, to be taken to the coroner's office, and then the arduous task began of trying to ascertain who the man was and how he had ended up dead in the canal. Officers were dispatched to talk to passersby and people who lived along the canal, and divers to search the bottom of the canal closer to the lock in search of any paraphernalia that might have belonged to the victim and shed some more light on the circumstances of his demise.

While her uncle and Chase oversaw the proceedings, she returned to the car to dispatch her own team of researchers in the form of her four cats. Their mission brief was clear: talk to any pet witnesses who might have seen something, and more specifically try to determine if foul play was involved or if the death of their John Doe was simply the consequence of a tragic accident.

Chapter Four

After Odelia had given us her instructions on how to contribute to her and Chase's investigation, I had to check my first impulse to spring into action. Instead, I patiently waited for Harriet to issue her own directives as to how to proceed. She was, after all, in charge now. At first, she didn't seem to grasp the significance, for she simply continued to groom herself and seemed oblivious that her troops were awaiting her command. Then, when three pairs of eyes

EXCERPT FROM PURRFECT GUITAR (MAX 80)

followed her every move, she finally seemed to realize that something was expected of her and said, "What are you waiting for? Didn't you hear what Odelia said? Let's get a move on, you guys. Hop to it, and be quick about it!"

"But… what do you want us to do, exactly?" asked Dooley.

"Odelia said to investigate, so let's investigate," she said.

"But… investigate what, exactly?" Dooley insisted.

Harriet rolled her eyes. "Do I have to spell it out for you? How about some initiative? Some enterprise? Some imagination!" She waved an impatient paw in the direction of the canal lock. "Just go forth and be fruitful, will you?"

I fully expected her to add 'and multiply,' but she stopped short of doing so. Instead, she started licking her impressive tail, making sure it looked just so. Clearly, she was intending to adopt a paws-off approach to her personal leadership style that would see her paw soldiers do all the actual paw-work. It was one way of doing things, of course, and who was I to offer any criticism? So instead, Dooley, Brutus, and I toddled off in the direction of the lock.

"What does Harriet mean by being fruitful, Max?" asked Dooley.

"Far be it from me to interpret our fearless leader's words, Dooley," I said. "But as I see it, she probably wants us to go out there and find clues."

"Clues and potential witnesses," Brutus clarified. "Anyone who saw something or heard something or smelled something. Anything at all."

"Oh, I see," said Dooley, though I could tell that he didn't. Not really.

We had arrived at the spot where the body of the dead man had been found floating. No doubt the current had tried to take it past the lock but had seen its progress hampered by the man-made construction, causing the body to thunk against the sturdy wooden doors that had been built to regulate the difference in water level so that boats could safely navigate the canal. Judging from the state of the body, that thunking had gone on for a little while, giving it a decidedly careworn aspect and reducing it to a shadow of its former self.

The lock itself was an impressive feat of engineering, and we got there just in time to see a diver submerging himself into the murky waters of the canal to look for possible clues as to the presence of a dead man in that spot—though what Uncle Alec was hoping to find was beyond me. Then again, possibly this was standard procedure when a waterlogged body was found on the Chief's watch.

Mayor Butterwick, the Chief's wife, had also arrived, and her face registered concern. I could see why. Like a lot of Hamptons towns, Hampton Cove caters to the tourist trade, and it's never a good look for any town trying to attract that kind of business to suddenly start dragging waterlogged corpses from canals. It's not what most people are looking for when selecting a holiday destination.

"Charlene doesn't look happy, Max," said Dooley, who had noticed the same phenomenon. "Why is that, you think?"

"Yeah, do you think there's trouble in paradise, Max?" asked Brutus, referring to the fact that Uncle Alec and Charlene had recently tied the knot.

"I think Charlene's concern is strictly connected to the fact that no mayor likes to see their town get any bad press," I said. "It might attract a species of person called the disaster tourist, and nobody wants to have those around."

"And why is that?" asked Dooley. "Isn't any tourist a good tourist?"

"Not when all they want is to snap pictures of dead people and post them on their social media," I said. "It sends the wrong message, and might lead to bad publicity for this lovely town of ours."

EXCERPT FROM PURRFECT GUITAR (MAX 80)

"Oh, I see," said Dooley, nodding. "People want sun and surf when they come to the Hamptons, not death and decay and rotting corpses."

I grimaced. "Something like that."

"Nicely put, Dooley," Brutus murmured. He sighed. "So where do we begin? I don't see any pets around, you guys. No dogs or cats as far as I can tell."

He was right. Which led me to assume that perhaps Harriet had wanted us to talk to the non-pet variety of species, of which I was sure there would be plenty. Birds, for one thing, like to go for the bird's eye view and can generally be relied upon to be excellent witnesses. Or the bugs that live in the high grass that covers the bank of the canal and offer the worm's eye view. Or even the ducks that my eagle eye could spot. "Why don't we go and talk to those guys over there?" I suggested.

Brutus took one look at those ducks and made a face. "I don't like ducks," he confessed. And I could see where he was coming from. Once upon a time he had fallen foul of a group of ducks in our local park when he accidentally ended up in the duck pond. It had put him off ducks for good. But since a sleuth worth his or her salt never lets their personal hang-ups stand in the way of good detective work, we set paw in the direction of our feathered friends anyway.

"You do the talking, Max," said Brutus. "And if they come too close, I'm out of here—is that understood?"

"Absolutely," I said. "Though I wouldn't worry about these ducks becoming aggressive, Brutus. They look the peaceable kind."

"And how would you know?" he grumbled. "They look pretty nasty to me."

We approached the ducks in a rather stealthy way, since a lot of ducks like to take flight the moment they see a cat come anywhere near them, and we didn't want that kind of thing happening now—not when they might prove to be valuable witnesses in our ongoing inquiries.

"Hey there, ducks," I said by way of greeting, since we weren't on a first-name basis yet.

The ducks gave me a dirty look. "What do you want, cat?" asked one of them, possibly the leader. There were three of them in all, and this one was a male, judging from its plumage.

"Yeah, what do you want, cat?" asked a second duck, a female this time.

"We just want to ask you a couple of questions," I said.

"We don't buy from strangers," said the male duck.

"Yeah, whatever it is you're selling, we don't want it," said his friend.

"We're not trying to sell you anything," I assured the ducks. "We just want to ask you about the dead man that was dragged from the canal just now."

"Dead man? What dead man?" asked the male duck.

"I didn't see no dead man," said the second duck.

It was at this moment that the third duck piped up. It seemed younger than the others, and could have been a duckling, or perhaps it was simply small for its age—I admit I'm not a fowl expert. "I saw the dead man," said this duck or duckling. "My name is Philip, by the way—what's yours?"

"Max," I said. "And these are my friends Brutus and Dooley."

"Philip, don't say another word," said the male duck.

"Oh, Dad, these are nice cats," said Philip. And to us: "Don't mind my folks. They're old-fashioned and don't like cats for some reason."

"There's a very good reason we don't like cats!" said the dad. "Remember what happened to your uncle Henry? He almost lost a limb because of a cat attack. Don't come any closer!" he suddenly yelled when I took a step in his direction. "I'm warning you, cat—I've got a gun and I won't hesitate to use it!"

I wondered where the duck could possibly be concealing a gun, and so I figured he just might be bluffing. I decided not to call his bluff, though, and took a couple of steps back instead. "So you saw the dead man?" I asked the kid.

Philip nodded fervently. "I saw him floating around." He made a face. "He smelled funny so I decided to give him a wide berth. Do all humans smell funny, Max?"

"Only if they've been dead a while," I assured the youngster.

"Or if they're not very big on personal hygiene," Brutus murmured. He was eyeing the ducks closely, just in case they got up to any funny business. Likewise, the ducks were eyeing us with distinct suspicion—mindful of what had happened to this Uncle Henry of theirs.

"Did you happen to see the dead man before he ended up in the canal?" I asked.

Philip thought hard about that one. "I'm not sure," he finally admitted. "Humans all look the same to me. If you've seen one, you've seen them all."

"True," said his mom.

The kid shrugged. "I just figured this particular human had gone for a swim and liked it so much he decided to keep on swimming."

"That's an awfully long swim," his dad scoffed.

"I'll say," Brutus grunted.

"Humans like to go for swims," said Philip defensively. "Remember that guy a couple of days ago? Even you said he was crazy, Dad."

"That's true," the dad admitted. When I gave him a quizzical look, he elaborated, "We get our fair share of swimmers here, but this guy took the cake."

"He must have been in there for hours," said his wife.

"Kept diving and coming up for air as if it was some fancy schmancy pool and not a smelly canal."

"Would you say the canal is smelly?" asked her husband.

"I would," his wife confirmed. "It's very smelly, and you know it. And if you were anything like your brother Henry, you would have taken us out of here a long time ago."

"It's not as easy as that," the duck grumbled.

"There's a perfectly nice pond in the park," said his wife. "My sister lives there with her kids, and she keeps telling me it's a regular paradise compared to this awful canal."

"The pond is full," said her husband gruffly.

"It's not full! There's plenty of space for an enterprising duck who's prepared to show some initiative!" She rolled her eyes. "My mother warned me against you. But did I listen?"

"Dad doesn't like Grandpa and Grandma," Philip whispered. "And they don't like him."

"I like them perfectly fine," said his dad huffily. "But they've poisoned all the other ducks' minds against me. Can I help it I wasn't born in Hampton Cove but in Hampton Keys?"

"It's got nothing to do with that, and you know it," said his wife. "The fact of the matter is that you feel too good to mingle with the other ducks. Just because you were born in a mansion owned by a famous pop star, you think you're better than the rest of us."

"Were you really born in a mansion, Dad?" asked Philip.

"I was," said his dad proudly. "A mansion owned by none other than Charlie Dieber."

The three of us shared a look of dismay. We had made Charlie Dieber's acquaintance in a distant past, and the experience hadn't been a happy one, to say the least.

"So why don't we move back there?" asked Philip.

"Ask your mom," said the duck unhappily.

"Hampton Cove is where I was born and raised, and I will

EXCERPT FROM PURRFECT GUITAR (MAX 80)

not leave my family," said Philip's mom decidedly. "And there will be no more talk about moving to Hampton Keys—is that understood?"

"Yes, Mom," said Philip obediently.

"There's a good duck," she said.

Philip gave me a wink. "Once I'm big enough, I'll go exploring," he whispered. "Take a look at this Charlie Dieber's mansion for myself and meet my dad's family. It'll be grand!"

I could have told him that he was in for a big disappointment, but since I believe that every person—or duck—should be allowed to decide their own fate, I wisely kept my tongue.

"So about that swimmer," I said, trying to steer the conversation back in a more productive direction.

"Oh, right," said Philip. "Well, he spent all day in the water, and then he came back the next day and did the same thing. So I kinda expected him to show up a third day in a row, and when he didn't, I kinda felt a little sad—I'd gotten used to having him around by then."

"Could he be the dead person you saw floating around in there?" I asked.

Philip nodded slowly. "I'm not sure. It's possible, of course."

"With humans, you can expect anything," said his mom. "They're tricky." She was looking at her husband as she said it, and I had a feeling she wasn't referring to the mystery swimmer.

"I like Charlie Dieber," said Philip's dad defiantly. "A gentleman and friend to ducks."

"Just because he liked to throw you the odd piece of bread doesn't make him a good person," said his wife. She sighed heavily. "You are entirely too gullible, Marcus."

"And you are entirely too critical, Martha," he shot back. "Charlie is fine."

"Well, if he's so fine, why did you move to Hampton Cove, huh?"

"I followed my heart," he said.

She softened a little. "Oh."

"Love does that."

"Oh?"

"Don't mind them," said Philip. "Grandma says they're passionate. And Grandpa says they're pre… prespo… presposterous. I wouldn't know, since I'm just a duckling."

I smiled. "I think you're a very clever duckling, Philip. And I want to thank you for telling us about that swimmer. When would you say you saw him?"

"Oh… about three days ago maybe? Grandma came over for a visit—she does that every week—so it must have been Tuesday, since that's her regular day."

"Heaven forbid she would skip a week," Marcus murmured.

"Anything else you can tell us about the swimmer?" I asked.

Philip thought hard. "Well… he wasn't alone. There was a woman with him. She didn't go into the water, though, but stayed on shore while the man was in the canal. Oh, and she was on her phone the whole time. But then most humans are on their phones the whole time."

"What did she look like, this woman?" I asked.

"Um, small and cute and blond," said Philip.

"And what would you know about that?" said his mother, much dismayed.

"I may be a duckling, but I have eyes in my head, Mom," said the precocious youngster. "She was petite."

"Petite!" said his dad, throwing up his wings.

But the kid was not impressed. "Petite and blond and cute and her name was…" He thought some more, then finally brightened. "Hannah! At least that's what the man called her every time he dredged something up from the canal and deposited it on shore. And she called him…" More thinking ensued, which finally yielded a result. "Doug! That's right. Doug and Hannah. I remember thinking they had funny names. He was very handsome, by the way. Like a movie star. And so was she. Two movie stars frolicking in the canal—or at least he frolicked. She, not so much."

And now he was dead—at least if it was the same man. So no more frolicking would ensue. We thanked Philip profusely, said our goodbyes to Martha and Marcus, and took our leave, safe in the knowledge that we had gleaned some great clues—possibly even the identity of the dead man.

ABOUT NIC

Nic has a background in political science and before being struck by the writing bug worked odd jobs around the world (including but not limited to massage therapist in Mexico, gardener in Italy, restaurant manager in India, and Berlitz teacher in Belgium).

When he's not writing he enjoys curling up with a good (comic) book, watching British crime dramas, French comedies or Nancy Meyers movies, sampling pastry (apple cake!), pasta and chocolate (preferably the dark variety), twisting himself into a pretzel doing morning yoga, going for a brisk walk, and spoiling his feline assistants Lily and Ricky.

He lives with his wife (and aforementioned cats) in a small village smack dab in the middle of absolutely nowhere and is probably writing his next 'Mysteries of Max' book right now.

www.nicsaint.com

Printed in Great Britain
by Amazon